GOING

to

the

Dogs

Jay Heavner

Canaveral Publishing

Cover design by Chris Stanley

Fineline Printing, Titusville, Florida

All the author's books can be obtained at Amazon

Braddock's Gold Novels

Braddock's Gold

Hunter's Moon

Fool's Wisdom

Killing Darkness

Florida Murder Mystery Novels

Death at Windover

Murder at the Canaveral Diner

Murder at the Indian River

Murder at Seminole Pond

Murder of Cowboy Gene

Murder in the Family

Murder the Most Dangerous Game

Going to the Dogs

Dedication

To

Pet Owners everywhere who have ever rescued a pet and then had that pet steal their heart away.

Acknowledgments

Special thanks to my wife, Vivian

for suggestions, proofing, support, and edition.

Thanks, William Rowland for first proofing.

To all my first readers,

Sandy Anne Smith,

Rene Hunt,

Marie Waters Clyne,

Cindy Moran,

Janice Carey

Ann Tayloe

and,

Ashley Marang

Chapter 1

Late Fall 1987

Roger should have known it wasn't going to be a normal, ordinary day when he saw the elephant running down the road in front of his old trailer. No, even this was out of the ordinary for the quirky little town of Canaveral Flats, Florida. The trumpeting of the pachyderm got his attention as well as K9 his dog, Patches the cat, and Donkey, what else... a donkey.

Roger hurriedly got out of his La-Z-Boy chair and stood gawking in disbelief as the large gray tusker thundered by. Donkey loped to the fence gate and brayed. The cat just stared, and K9 barked, whimpered, and turned her head toward Roger in a questioning manner. "Yeah, K9, I see it, too. And it's not pink. I'm glad I cut down drinkin', so I know I'm not hallucinatin'. Even in my bad days back then, I never saw pink elephants. That thing's real. We can believe our eyes."

At a discrete distance, several vehicles with flashing lights but no sirens followed. The first was a Brevard County Sheriff's sedan and then a Florida Wildlife and Fish Commission truck. Next came a Florida Highway Patrol car, Canaveral Flats Chief of Police Bill Kenney in his truck, a Brevard County Animal Control truck, and in the rear, a panel truck with Price's Family Circus painted on the side.

1

"Well, K9, I believe it would be safe to assume one of the elephants from the circus in town's escaped and has about one-half of the county's law enforcement in hot pursuit. I fear this isn't goin' to end well."

K9 barked and wagged her tail.

"Yeah, we can only hope."

The aberration soon passed, and things got back to normal. Roger kicked back in his La-Z-Boy chair, and the cat jumped on his lap. K9 wanted attention, too, and Roger stroked her head. "Good girl," he said, "good girl."

Donkey moseyed through the yard and seemed to be heading toward the backside of the trailer where the water-filled ditch was. He disappeared from view. Roger stroked the fur of the cat and dog. He closed his eyes and nearly drifted off, but a bark from K9 brought him back to reality. A very expensive gold automobile stopped in front of his trailer.

"I wasn't expectin' anyone today, K9. Is this one of your friends comin' to visit? From the car, could be a Rolls. It looks more like the crowd you hang out with, not me."

K9 barked an affirmative.

"Now, don't get any airs about you. I know about your humble beginnin'."

She barked again.

A black man in a chauffeur's suit got out, opened the back door of the automobile, and a short woman wearing an elaborate dress that came nearly to the ground got out. She had a haughty hat with a large feather, the kind that had gone out of style decades ago, and in her hand, she held a lit cigarette with a long holder, one like

Audrey Hepburn carried in the movie, *Breakfast at Tiffany's*. They walked to the gate, and the man climbed over.

Roger yelled, "It's dummy-locked." He turned to K9. "Looks like we have visitors."

The black man opened the gate, and the woman confidently walked through it and headed down the path to Roger's ancient trailer. She carefully walked around the numerous pies the donkey had left in the driveway.

Roger turned and saw Donkey coming around the trailer. He walked toward the approaching couple. Roger said, "Donkey, they're guests and are to be treated kindly. You be on your best behavior if you know what's good for you."

Donkey paid him as much notice as he usually does, none. He walked right up to the lady, who stopped and held her cane in front of her with both hands. "Stop there, young man. That's close enough."

To Roger's surprise, he did just that. She reached into her purse for something, placed it in her hand, and presented it to Donkey, who took it with his dexterous lips and then swallowed it. He cooed. She stepped forward and placed her hand on his neck. "Good donkey. Aren't you a sweetie? Good donkey." She turned to the black man. "Come, James. We have business to attend to."

"Yes, ma'am."

The pair walked to Roger's trailer. He got out of his chair and said, "I'm Roger Pyles, and who do I have the pleasure of welcoming today to my humble abode?"

"My name is Mrs. Gladys Porcher. The name's spelled p o r c h e r, but it's pronounced por-shay. My husband's ancestors came from France. And this is my chauffeur, James."

He said, "Very pleased to meet you, sir."

She said, "We've heard so much about you, Mr. Pyles. May we come in?"

"Sure, and please call me Roger. Mr. Pyles seems so formal."

"Very well," she said.

James opened the screen door, and they walked into the screened porch. K9 greeted them.

Roger said, "K9, be considerate to our guests."

Mrs. Porcher smiled. "I'm so glad you have a dog for a pet." She stroked K9's head. "Good dog."

"She's not the only one. I have a cat that usually hides from strangers, and a donkey. He was a foundling I took in for a short time that's become an extended stay. Won't you take a seat?" He pointed to the two lawn chairs sitting side by side on the porch. "It may not be what you're used to, but it's what I got."

She said, "They'll be adequate. Thank you."

Roger said, "Can I get you something to drink? I have soft drinks, bottled water, beer, and I think I still have a little wine. What would you like?"

She said, "The wine sounds interesting. James, what will you have?"

"Do you have root beer?"

"A&W."

"That will be fine."

Roger said, "Comin' right up."

He went into the trailer, got an iced tea for himself which he stuck in his back pocket, and grabbed a root beer. Yes, he had a half-full bottle of wine, some Mogen David 20/20. He wasn't sure how long it had been there or how it got there. He poured some in a paper cup, filling it to an inch from the brim, and then carried it out to his guests.

"Here you go." He handed the drinks out. "I hope the wine's suitable."

They thanked him and took a sip. James smiled and nodded his approval. Mrs. Porcher's face drew up. Roger wasn't sure if she was surprised or disgusted or both. "Is it satisfactory, Mrs. Porcher?"

"Dear me. I haven't had anything like this since my college days. Does it bring back memories. Mad Dog 20/20. That's a taste you don't forget. I can't say it will ever be my favorite, but I believe in accepting whatever my host provides. Thank you for your hospitality, Roger."

"You're welcome."

"You're probably wondering why I came out here today unannounced. I tried to call, but your phone seemed out of service."

He said, "I've had a lot of trouble with that phone. Can't ever seem to keep it workin'."

She said, "It's just as well. What I have is of utmost importance, and I'd rather discuss this delicate matter face to face. You see; I have this problem. It's a matter of life and death."

Chapter 2

Roger interrupted. "Could we stop right there and back up the truck, please? I don't know you from Adam's house cat, Mrs. Porcher. Could you tell me a little about yourself, and what brings you here today to my humble abode before you tell me your problem?"

From her expression, Roger saw she wasn't used to being interrupted and questioned. The sour face disappeared as she swallowed a little bit of her pride. "Very well, Mr. Pyles. I do seem to have gotten the cart before the horse." She paused, as if thinking. "It's come to my attention that you are an excellent sleuth and detective. Dare I say the best in the area? And I know you are selective in the cases you take. Despite your shabby appearances, you have little need for money or want for it, I've heard, though I am willing to reward you handsomely for your services. And speaking of handsome, you are quite so. You remind me of Sam Elliott, one of my favorite movie stars."

Roger shifted his position in the chair and said, "Okay, for the record, what kind of services are you in need of? My detective skills or somethin' else?"

She looked puzzled. "Something else? What could that be?"

Roger cleaned his throat. "I recently was in the Palm Beach area. While there, I heard stories of wealthy senior women who, well, would purchase the services of young men. Do you get my drift?"

Again, she looked puzzled. "No, I don't think I understand. State what you're trying to say in plain English."

A coy smile came to Roger's face. "Okay, are you shoppin' for a gigolo?"

Mrs. Porcher's mouth dropped open. "Why, Mr. Pyles, I'm shocked. Most certainly not! I should leave right now." She stopped. "But I need your services as a detective. Can we start over, Mr. Pyles?"

Roger thought he saw a suppressed grin on James's face, but he wasn't sure. "Okay, but it's Roger, Mrs. Porcher, not Mr. Pyles."

"Very well, Roger," she said.

"What's this life or death problem? What do you need my services as a detective for? What kind of trouble are you in?"

"It's of a delicate nature. You see, my dog, Tricki Woo, has disappeared. I shall just die if I don't get him back."

"Wait, Tricki Woo, like the dog in the BBC TV show, *All Creatures Great & Small*?"

She said, "Yes, that Tricki Woo. After seeing the show, I had to have a Pekingese, and my Tricki has lived up to his namesake's reputation and more. And he's disappeared. He means the world to me. My heart's broken, and I need him back. Money is of no object. I want him back, and will and can spare no means to get him back to me. Roger, I usually get my way no questions asked, but I'm begging you, please help me get my Tricki Woo back. Please."

Roger noted James had a surprised look on his face, but he did his best to suppress it. Roger shifted in his chair. He said nothing as he considered her offer. Here was this wealthy old grand dame in front of him pleading like her life depended on it. She'd not said a word about having to maneuver her way through his yard full of donkey pies. A question came to his mind. "Tell me, how did you know how to deal with Donkey?"

"Oh, that was easy. I've had to deal with many asses in my life, some with four legs and some with two, like my late husband. Experience is a hard teacher. You get the test before the training, but I passed and remember it very well."

Roger smiled. *She's one tough old bird. I think I could learn to like her, maybe, but she could be a real pain to deal with at times, which could be often.* He considered his options. *Perhaps I should help her. I could use a break from another gruesome case with guns and dead bodies. This could be what I need. Could it be that hard or dangerous to find a missing dog? Hard? Probably not. Or dangerous? Probably not. But you never know. Why not take it?* Roger couldn't think of a good reason why not.

"Okay, I'll help, but there'll be certain circumstances."

"Like what, Roger?"

"I'll need you to be completely straightforward with me. I'll need to talk to your help and family in confidence, and you're not to interfere or hold anything they say against them, understand?"

She nodded. "I was expecting as much. I don't like it, but I want my Tricki Woo back. What else? I know there's more."

"I may need to look at your finances and business interest for a motive and suspect."

She said, "I expected as much. I called Animal Services for help. They said they didn't have the ability to search for a lost dog. They only answered calls from county residents about animals in the flesh. They were not proactive. I went to the police, and they said they looked for lost people, not pets and, they were stretched thin on that. I talked to private detectives, and they weren't interested, no matter how much money I offered. So, Roger, I'm desperate. I'm willing to compensate you royally to look for my Tricki Woo. Please, Roger, please help me."

Roger studied her. He could see no guile in her eyes. She truly was at the end of her rope. He felt his heart going out for the old lady. Perhaps he could help. "Okay, I'm in, but, under those circumstances, I mentioned."

She sighed. "Oh, thank you, Roger. I've been losing sleep and weight over this. You don't know what it means to me. What kind of compensation do you want? Anything."

"Cover my expenses and ten percent plus an hourly rate of $40 per hour if I find him or not. If I bring him back alive and well, I'll let you decide any additional compensation you feel is fitting."

"That's more than fair, very reasonable. Young man, I have faith in you. I know you **will** bring him back to me alive and well."

"I hope so, Mrs. Porcher. That's the plan, but you never know. You must be prepared for all possibilities."

"We won't go there, Roger. Think positive. You will get my Tricki back safe and sound."

"Okay, let's start right now. I need to talk to James. And in private." He saw a hint of reluctance in her eyes, but she agreed. "Good. We're gettin' off to a positive start."

Jay Heavner

"I'd like him to walk me to my car first before you talk. Is that alright?"

"That would be fine," Roger said. "We can get started when he gets back."

" Very good," she said. "James, I need a little help. I've sat too long in this low chair and am not sure I can get out without help. Would you please help me?"

"Yes, ma'am."

He helped her up. "These old legs aren't what they used to be. James, let's go. Thank you for your hospitality and taking up my offer. I can almost see my Tricki running up to greet me now."

Roger said, "I'll do my best, Mrs. Porcher."

"I have every confidence in you." She paused. "Oh, there is one more thing you should know. Tricki wore a collar with diamonds on it. If I get it back, fine. If not, also fine. I want my Tricki back. He's worth more than diamonds to me. Come, James, let's go. Goodbye."

"Goodbye to you, too."

Roger watched as they walked down the dirt driveway to her car. James helped her in it, and he soon returned to Roger's trailer. Roger said, "So, you're James. I have a bunch of questions for you."

James smiled. "I'll bet you do."

Chapter 3

"James, I'd like you to be as candid as you can be with me. Everything you tell me will be confidential, and if I hear that Mrs. Porcher gets on your case about what you tell me, I'm off the case. That's not an idle threat. The way I read her is she's at the end of her rope on this matter, and she'll do about anything to get her Tricki Woo back. Is my assessment of the current situation correct or not? You know her far better than I do, I suspect," Roger said.

James smiled. "I believe you are correct, sir."

"None of this sir stuff. It's Roger, plain old Roger."

"Okay, Roger, you're assessment is correct. Mrs. Porcher loves that dog, probably more than anything else in this world. I was surprised by how easily she gave in to your requests. She usually drives a hard bargain, just because she can, and I believe she enjoys it, sir."

"That doesn't surprise me at all, and I thought I said none of this sir stuff."

James smiled, revealing a mouthful of pearly white teeth that contrasted his brown skin. "It's hard not to do. It was how my daddy raised me. He served in the military, and when I came of age, he advised me to go in. I did. Served for five years and came out with a DD 214 and all my GI benefits. Everything there was, Yes, Sir, No, Sir, and it's a habit I don't even think about."

Roger said, "I grew up in hardscrabble West Virginia and many a young man from there used the military as a ticket out and a better life. I got a scholarship to college and took the education route out."

"What brought you to Florida?" James asked.

"I was tryin' to escape my problems and start out anew."

"That's the history of this state. Seems like everyone came from someplace else or their ancestors did. I can't trace my family tree back any further than the Civil War. They were illiterate slaves until the Emancipation Proclamation. No one cared to collect that information back then, and Massa on the plantation didn't want it written down. Poor, illiterate people who don't know their history are easier to control."

"Very true," Roger said.

"I think I'm mixed race. I'm bald and balding is something that started in white folk. Guess there was a white boy in the woodpile somewhere."

Roger laughed as did James. The latter continued, "Some people don't want to talk about it, but there was a lot of mixing going on. A lot of the labor around the plantation were half-breed kids of one white plantation owner and slave girls that got sold and farmed out to neighboring plantations."

Roger said, "I've heard some stories about that, but I need to get back to the Tricki Woo problem. Mrs. Porcher will be wonderin' what's keeping us."

"Very well. It's a subject I believe needs brought to light. Now, what do you need to know about the Tricki Woo problem?"

"What do you think happened to him? Did he get dognapped? Did he get lost or run away? Are there people out there that would want to take him? What about the valuable collar? Does Mrs. Porcher have any enemies?"

James said, "That's a lot of questions."

"It is. Right now, I'm short on answers and need to figure out what happened."

James put his hand to his chin and stroked it. "What happened to Tricki Woo? I don't know. I wasn't there that day. I was with my family. When I got home, I found a message on my answering machine from Mrs. Porcher. She was frantic. I rushed right over and found her crying. She looked like she'd been doing that for quite a while. Her eyes were all red, and tears stained her cheeks.

"It took some time to get her calmed down and able to answer questions. I finally got it out of her that Tricki Woo was missing. She'd put him out to do his business in the yard, and when she came out later to let him in, he wasn't anywhere to be found. She searched all over the yard and house before she called me and left the message.

"I came over and searched the whole place that evening, too, but no Tricki Woo. All I found was a dogpile he'd left. Her yard's fenced, but a dog his size could get out if he wanted to, and with a little effort, if motivated. I do handyman work around her property besides being her driver. I told her the fence needed fixing, but she kept putting it off. She's tight, too tight for her own good. She's so tight it's a wonder she don't squeak sometimes. It surprised me how easy she was willing to part with her money to get him back. That lonely old lady wants her dog back bad."

Roger asked, "What about the collar? That complicates things."

"It does, but I wouldn't worry about the collar too much. You find the dog, return him safely, and you'll make Mrs. Porcher very happy."

"Interesting. Did you expand the search?" Roger asked.

"I did, but it had poured rain, and I could find no trail or what had become of Tricki Woo. He'd vanished. Disappeared. Gone without a trace."

"So, do you think he took off?"

James said, "I don't know. Could be."

"Could someone have taken him?"

"That could be, too. He was a happy camper that never met a person he didn't like. Same with other dogs. About the only thing he didn't like were some big tomcats and chickens. He'd go after them and get pecked. I cleaned out several of his wounds from the neighbor's chickens. He and a big pecker rooster disliked each other intensely, but they usually stayed away from each other."

Roger asked, "Does she have any enemies?"

"A few, but no more than most of the old-money rich families in the area. It's possible, I guess. Someone could want to part her with some of her money to get her dog back. It could be."

"Any family issues I should know about?"

James said, "Her husband died about ten years ago. She has a son and a daughter and some extended family."

"What about her children?" Roger said.

He laughed. "They're an interesting lot. Hugh, the son's a no-good playboy who's never worked an honest day in his life. He gets a big monthly stipend, and he lives it up until the money's gone, then he does whatever he has to, but as little as possible, to survive. Would he take the dog to get a big payout and endanger his monthly sure thing? It's not outside the realm of possibilities, but I don't know."

"How about the daughter?" Roger asked.

"I doubt it. She and her mother were never close, but I don't think she'd take the dog. Mrs. Porcher, as I said, came from old money, this Southern aristocracy. She wanted the daughter to be a Deb, kind of like Scarlett O'Hara, but that wasn't Bridget. She was a tomboy through and through. Seemed like Bridget and her mom were always fussin' at each other for one thing or another."

"Where can I find them?"

James said, "Bridget has a small farm out on Pluckebaum Road west of Cocoa where she spends most of her time. You should find her out there. Now, the son, God only knows where you'll find him. He's what you call a rolling stone. Wherever he lays his hat's his home. Good luck with that."

Roger nodded. "Well, you've given me a place to start. Wish I had more, but you have to go to war with the army you have."

"Yep, that's about the truth of it, Roger. If you need more information, I think you know where to find me. Now, I better be getting back in chauffeur mode. I'm sure Mrs. Porcher is antsy and will have a whole bunch of questions about what we talked about. Sometimes working for her is like walking a tight wire in the windstorm."

"I kinda got that impression, but I'm sure you'll do well with your cover story."

James smiled, "Old brain hasn't failed me yet."

Roger laughed. "You better get goin'." He rose from his chair and stuck out his hand. "Pleasure to talk with you, James. I may need to call on you again."

James shook his hand. "Happy to be of help. I got to get going. Bye."

"One more question. Can you think of anyone else I might want to talk to about this caper?"

"Yeah, the neighbors and Betty. I can't believe I forgot Betty."

Roger asked, "Who's Betty?"

"Betty's the housekeeper. She was there the day Tricki disappeared."

"Thanks, that helps a lot."

"I have to go. See you later. Bye."

Roger said, "I'll be in touch. Bye."

Roger watched as James walked down the driveway. He opened and closed the gate, walked to the Rolls, and got in. It did a U-turn and disappeared, going east on Canaveral Flats Boulevard.

Roger sat down in his La-Z-Boy chair. K9 emerged from the hole in the trailer skirting and went to Roger, who stroked her head. "Good girl. Good girl. What have I done? What do I know about finding an old lady's lost pet?"

K9 barked.

"Thanks for the vote of confidence. I could use one. Are you gonna help me?"

She barked again.

"I thought you would. Lost dogs are near and dear to your heart. Got any bloodhound in you?"

She wagged her tail.

"That's what I thought. Now, where to start? The game is afoot, as Shakespeare would say."

Chapter 4

Pow! Pow! Pow! A momentary pause followed with more gunfire, much more gunfire.

Roger said, "K9, I was afraid it wasn't goin' to end well."

She wagged her tail and whined.

Roger went inside and put a TV dinner in the microwave. Three minutes later, he pulled it out, grabbed a plastic fork, and headed for his La-Z-Boy chair. As he finished eating, a truck pulled up in front of his trailer and stopped.

"Grrr."

"Yeah, K9, it's your favorite flatfoot, Chief of Police Bill Kenney."

"Grrr."

"Behave yourself, K9. I need to talk to him. No bitin'. He'll leave a foul taste in your mouth."

She growled again, went through the hole in the trailer skirting, and disappeared.

Bill made his way through the dummy-locked gate and walked down to Roger's trailer. As he got near, Roger said, "Intruder alert. Release the hounds."

Bill laughed. "Where's K9?" A grrr came from under the trailer. "And hello to you, too, K9. How's that no-good Roger treating you?" She growled again. "That bad. Well then. I'll just have to make myself at home. Got any beer?"

"You know where the beer is, you big galoot. Get me one, too, and then tell me what happened."

"Sure thing." Bill went into the trailer and soon returned with two beers. "Here you go, buddy, and you don't even have to say thank you."

"Bill, you could try the patience of Job."

"That's an improvement. I'm usually told I could piss off the Pope."

"Whatever," Roger said. "Sit down and tell me what happened. I heard all the shootin'."

"The elephant had to be put down. I wish there was some other option, but someone was going to get hurt if we didn't."

"I was afraid of that."

"Yeah, one of the circus tents, where they stored hay, caught fire, and the elephant was right next to it. It was either stay there and become a cooked elephant or escape. The only thing holding him was a skinny rope tied to a wooden stake driven into the ground. Once an elephant finds how flimsy the ties are that bind him, it's almost impossible to hold him."

Roger said, "How so?"

"The circus people explained it to me. When the elephant is young, he's chained to a steel post embedded in concrete. He tries to get away, but no matter how he bellows and pulls, he can't get away,

19

so finally, he gives up and accepts it. Then he grows up, but he always remembers when he couldn't get away. All the circus has to do is rope him to a stake, and he'll stay put. He's quite capable of gaining his freedom, but he's still in the prison of his mind. Once he realizes this, there's no holding him back."

"So he becomes a danger to anyone and anything he encounters."

Bill said, "That's about the long and short of it. There was no containing him now. He had to be put down. Sad, but better than have someone trampled to death."

"I guess so. I heard a lot of shootin'."

"Yeah, our puny little handguns barely fazed him. The circus had a British .303 rifle that they carried just in case they had an emergency like this. The circus rifleman told me that during WW II, it was sometimes used to pierce metal as in tanks."

Roger said, "From the sound, I could tell it was a high-powered rifle being fired. Still sad they had to put him down."

"It is. Now they're trying to figure out what to do with several tons of dead elephant. Too bad we're not in a third-world country with a hungry village nearby. The natives would take care of it for us, but this is the good ole Brevard County, Florida, US of A."

"So what are they gonna do?"

Bill said, "Probably get a crane, hoist the carcass up on a flatbed, and take it to the landfill for burial."

"Such a sad end to a magnificent creature."

"It is, but what're you going to do?"

"I know. Don't seem right." Roger took a sip of his beer. "Bill, you might be able to help me with a situation."

"You know me. Always willing to help."

Roger gave him a quick sideways look and then said, "I had a special guest today and presented me with a peculiar problem."

"Who was it, the President?"

"No."

"The Governor?"

"Wrong again, but warmer," said Roger.

"Who then?"

"Do you know a Mrs. Gladys Porcher from Cocoa?"

"I know of her. She's kind of an eccentric old lady that comes from old money. Everyone calls her Happy Bottom when she's not around."

"Happy bottom?" Roger asked.

"Yeah. Gladys, glad ass. Get it?"

"Now, I'm with you."

"So what's her problem and how does it concern you?"

Roger said, "She lost her dog and wants me to find it for her."

Bill laughed. "Gee, I was thinking of all kinds of things it could be."

"I did, too, in the beginnin'. And she stated she would compensate me royally for my special help."

"So, what did you tell her?"

"I told her a definite maybe leaning toward yes. Do you think I did the right thing?"

Bill said, "It's up to you what you do. It could be interesting. I don't think you'll have too many people trying to kill you over a lost dog."

"He was wearing a diamond collar."

"Hmm. That complicated things a little. There's something else you should know about old money in the area. Some was gotten legitimate, some not so legit, and some, a little of both ways."

Roger asked, "What about her family?"

"I believe it was all above board, but you never know. Seems every family has a black sheep, skeletons in the closet, and a few secrets they'd like to keep quiet."

"I'll keep that in mind."

Bill said, "See? Always glad to be of service. Beer's done. Got to go. Duty calls. Bye." He rose from his chair and headed out the door.

"Alright. Thanks for the info. Come around again when you need a cold drink. Bye."

Bill smiled. "Will do."

Bill walked to his truck, and it soon disappeared down Canaveral Flats Boulevard going west.

"Well, K9. We got through another Bill encounter without the sheddin' of blood, so I guess it was successful." Roger thought for a moment. "What's my next move, K9? How 'bouts I..."

Chapter 5

Roger rode down US 1 in his truck. He stopped at a red light and saw a sign saying "Leaving Cocoa." Twenty feet past the light stood another sign: "Now entering Rockledge, Brevard County's Oldest City."

The light changed, and Roger drove on. A Sears Department store, a Food World grocery store, and an Eckerd's drug store were on the left. To the right was the Rockledge Railroad Station. It had definitely seen better times. He drove on for about a mile before turning left onto Barton Ave. St. Mary's Catholic Church stood on the right. It had a huge, impressive campus. A little further down the road was the original Catholic Church, a wooden building with a large historical marker in front that stated it was built in 1917. Roger proceeded down the sloping road until it dead-ended at Rockledge Drive. Across the street was the wide Indian River. He turned right, drove one block, and turned right onto a sandy narrow street, Oakwood Avenue. Mrs. Porcher's home was on the left.

He stopped the truck and admired the house and nicely landscaped area around it. Old spreading oak trees he guessed to be over a hundred years old shaped the property. A few tall native palms also graced the area. The English Tudor style house had a full porch across the front and a red shingle roof that accented the white house with its brown wooden trim. "About 4,000 square feet," he mumbled to himself. "Nice place."

He pulled into a sandy driveway in front of an outbuilding containing a one-car garage and what he assumed was a mother-in-law type apartment. It also had an English Tudor look. A large van with a sign that read, "Premium Pet Grooming," sat next to his vehicle. Roger got out and walked toward the back of the house, which seemed to be the most used route. As he passed a pool, he heard the back door of the house open and voices, but he couldn't make them out. He stopped and two women, one black and one white, approached talking. They stopped in their tracks when they saw Roger.

Roger smiled, "Sorry if I scared you. Would this be the home of Mrs. Gladys Porcher?"

The black woman spoke, "It is. You are whom, and what's your business?"

"I'm Roger Pyles. I had a visit from Mrs. Porcher earlier today, and she asked me about findin' her missin' dog, Tricki Woo. And who might you two lovely ladies be?"

They smiled, and he thought the black woman's face grow a little red. She spoke, "I'm Betty. I'm Mrs. Porcher's housekeeper."

The other woman spoke, "I'm Amy Hunter. I groom Tricki Woo. Make him look handsome, but it seems he's run away."

Betty said, "I better tell Mrs. Porcher you're here." She walked to the house and went in.

Amy said, "And I have to be going. Got other creatures that need my services."

Roger said, "Could I talk to you for a few moments, please, about Tricki Woo? It could be really helpful in findin' him."

"Okay. If it helps find him, sure. Why not?"

"Thanks. Let's grab a spot at that table over in the shade by the ool."

"By the ool?"

Roger said, "Yeah, see the sign." He pointed. "See, it says, 'There's no p in our ool. Let's keep it that way.'"

She laughed. "You know, as many times as I've been here, I never noticed that."

"Guess there's been some problems with that in the past. Let's get down to our business, and then you can get on to yours."

She smiled. "No need to rush, is there?"

"Only to find the missing pooch. You groomed Tricki. Tell me a little about him."

"He was one of a kind. Always happy, well, almost always. He'd get burrs in his fur and he didn't like when I had to work them out. Tricki didn't mind the baths, but was a little afraid of the hair dryer. Overall, he was a joy to work with. I wish they were all as easy as he was. Do you think you can find him and get him back to Mrs. Porcher?"

Roger said, "I have every intention of doin' that. Did he do anything odd or have any eccentricities?"

"Just normal dog stuff."

"Like what?"

"He liked to roll in things."

"Like?

"Anything with a bad or rotten smell. It drove Mrs. Porcher crazy. I'd get a call out of the blue. 'Come bathe my dog. He smells terrible. I can't let him in the house like this.' I'd work Tricki into my schedule. Of course, I'd charge her premium for dropping everything and coming over ASAP. Tricki's love of nasty smelling things sure put a lot of extra cash in my pocket. For that reason alone, I hope you get him back soon."

Roger laughed. "Yeah, I can see that. What else can you tell me that could be important?"

"He was a dirty dog."

"What do you mean?"

"He liked the girl dogs and if one wasn't available, he might just try to hump your leg. Mrs. Porcher loved that dog, but his behavior tried her patience some times."

Roger laughed. "Yeah, I get the picture. Mrs. Porcher has guests over, and Tricki comes along and does his thing on some lady's leg. That would be a riot to see. Why doesn't she have him fixed?"

"You'll have to ask her that. Oh, here she comes." Amy got up. "I think it's time for me to go." She handed him her business card. "If you need a pet groomed, or," she paused and winked one eye, "anything else, give me a call. Nice meeting you, Roger. Bye."

Roger grinned. "Yeah, bye."

Amy got in her truck and backed out onto Oakwood Street. It soon disappeared down the road by the Indian River.

"Roger, what brings you here so soon?"

"I need to check the area Tricki was last seen in. He may still be here. Mrs. Porcher, you forgot to tell me where you lived."

"Oh, dear. I'm so sorry. This matter about Tricki Woo has put my brain in a tizzy. It's a wonder I can think at all." She stopped. "Do you think you'll find him here?"

"Maybe, or some evidence as to where he's got off to. I need complete access to the grounds and every building on the property."

She said, "Start at the garage and the apartment. They're both open. Give me a few minutes to see the house is presentable, if you wouldn't mind, Roger."

"No problem at all, Mrs. Porcher. I'd like to start right now. The sooner I start, the better a chance of finding Tricki."

"And returning him to me."

"That's the idea."

"Then let's get to it. The house will be ready when you're done out here."

"That sounds like a plan."

"Then let's get with it."

Roger smiled, "Yes, ma'am. For Tricki."

She grinned. "Roger, you've given me hope. I was afraid I'd never see him again."

"I'll do my best for you."

She had a twinkle in her eyes. "I know you will for me and Tricki."

"Yes, ma'am." He headed toward the garage.

Chapter 6

Roger walked to his truck and got a flashlight. Just as she'd said, the building was not locked. There wasn't much to see other than work tools around the sides. A locked wooden box sat on the floor. It was big enough to hide a small dog, but the lid had cracks. He shined his light through the cracks, but saw no sign of Tricki. A car, also unlocked, occupied most of the space. He opened the driver's door and inspected the interior. No dog. Roger pulled the trunk release, and it popped open. No dog inside. He pulled the carpet up to check the tire space. No dog.

He went outside, walked to the apartment door, and knocked. No answer. He opened the door. "Hello. Anybody home? Hello?"

No answer. It didn't look like anyone had lived in the efficiency for a while. He checked the room, under the bed, the closet, and the bathroom. No Tricki.

He went outside and checked the fence around the yard he guessed to be about one-half acre. It was in pretty good shape, but sure enough, there were some spots where a small, determined dog could get out. Someone could have left a gate open, accidentally or not. That answered one of his questions. He could have run off, or been taken, or worse. There were still a lot of places around the house to find a missing dog, dead or alive.

He opened the gate and checked the wooded area behind the garage. Nothing. He walked down to the Indian River and checked the rough coquina rock bank from which the town got its name. No Tricki. No body. Nothing but a discarded beer bottle and a candy bar wrapper. From the street, he checked neighbor's yards for signs of the dog. Nothing.

Roger walked back to the house. Mrs. Porcher was waiting. "There you are, young man. I thought you'd gotten as lost as Tricki Woo. The house is tidied up now. You may come in and look around. Did you see any sign of him?"

"No, nothing. I'd like to start at the top and work my way down. It looks like you have a partial at grade finished basement."

"Yes, the rest is natural. There's plastic down as a vapor barrier, but it's dirty and nasty down there. You don't think Tricki would go there, do you? It's not a very civilized area."

"I'll need to check to eliminate the possibility. Dogs don't see nasty like you and I do."

"That's certainly the truth. Come Roger. I'll take you to the attic rooms. They're finished."

They went into the house through the back door and climbed a narrow set of stairs with winders all the way to the attic.

Mrs. Porcher puffed. "Goodness. I haven't done that in ages."

Roger said, "That was quite a climb. You got some good lungs there, Mrs. Porcher. I hope I can do that when I reach your age."

"I try to take care of myself. I've still got places to go and people to annoy. Look around all you want, just find my Tricki."

"No problem with looking through the cabinets or closets?"

"Anywhere you need to."

"Okay."

Roger checked the closets, dresser drawers, the small bathroom, the bed, and under it. Nothing. "Anything else to see up here?"

"There's access to the crawl space under the roof behind that dresser if you want to check."

"I do. We need to be thorough."

"Very well, but you'll have to move the dresser. It's a bit much for me."

"Okay." Roger moved it and opened a small door. "Man, it's hot in there."

Mrs. Porcher said. "I knew it would be. I don't think he could survive for long in there."

"I don't think so either, but we have to know for sure." Roger crawled on his hands and knees in the tight area. He shined his light in the dark areas, but there was no evidence Tricki Woo had ever been there. Roger backed out. He gasped. "Thought I was goin' to pass out."

"I told you it was hot. Please close it up and put the dresser back where it was."

He huffed. "Sure." He moved it back into its original spot. "Where to now?"

"There're three bedrooms on the second floor. Follow me."

They walked down the stairs.

31

"Nice floors. What kind of wood is it?" Roger asked.

"It's Merritt Island heart of pine. You won't find material like this anymore."

"That's for sure."

The rooms with 12-foot ceilings each had a fireplace and were lavishly furnished. The windows had stained glass transoms above them that let in a warm, soothing light.

"Time is of the essence, Roger. Aren't you supposed to be looking for Tricki, not gawking at the house?"

"Guess so. It's a little different from where I grew up or what I'm used to." He stopped. "This could take a while."

"Okay. Get on with it."

Roger felt his temper rising, but he suppressed it for Tricki Woo. He wanted to see the dog found safely. Roger went over the rooms, bathrooms, cabinets, and furniture with a fine-toothed comb. He took his good old time to see if he could irritate her like she had him.

"Must you take so long?" she asked.

Roger suppressed a grin. "I need to check every place a dog could fit in. I'd hate to think I took a shortcut, and missed him."

She grimaced. "Yes, we wouldn't want that. If you're done here, we can go to the first floor. It has a large hallway, a great room I use for entertaining, a kitchen, and dining room, a bedroom, and a bathroom. Take your time, but there're more places for him to be than on the second floor."

Roger smiled. "Sounds like a plan."

They went downstairs and Roger began his search. It was certainly a nice and well kept up home, but rather stuffy and over furnished. As Roger worked, Betty came in. She said, "Could I get something for you? Tea or water?"

"Water would be fine, thank you."

She left, and he went about his search, but again, no Tricki Woo. He was still missing. Roger went into the kitchen. Betty had bottled water waiting for him.

He asked, "Where's Mrs. Porcher?"

"I could tell you exacerbated her, and she went outside for a cigarette. She won't smoke in the house. She's been smoking pretty heavy since Tricki disappeared."

"Well, the feeling was mutual." He sat down and took a drink. "Thank you."

"She's not the easiest person to work for, but she pays well."

"I can imagine. She mentioned that I should question her kids about the whereabouts of Tricki. Can you think of anyone else I should talk to?"

"His vet comes to mind. Doctor Solomon has an office on Brevard Avenue, but Tricki was special. He made house calls here for Tricki. Of course, he charged extra for that. He liked Tricki, and Tricki liked him. Mrs. Porcher and him had a private meeting about Tricki recently, but I don't know what the issue was."

"Think I need to talk with the vet. Thanks for the drink. I need to get to work. I saw the door to the basement. You don't need to direct me. I can find my own way."

Betty said, "As you wish."

Roger went downstairs and did a close inspection, but found nothing unusual. A search in the crawlspace found nothing but cobwebs, dirt, and darkness. He nearly got tangled in some wires, but managed to escape. Roger opened a lattice door and pulled himself into the warm sunlight. He stood up and walked to the back of the house.

"Goodness," a voice exclaimed. "Roger, did you find Tricki? You look terrible!"

He looked at himself. "Yeah, guess I do. But no, no Tricki Woo. He's still missin'." He walked over to where she sat smoking her cigarette. "I need a breather."

"So, you searched the entire house from top to bottom and found nothing. What next?"

Roger said, "I'm goin' to look around the neighborhood, includin' the woods in the back. I hope I find him, but if I don't, I'll make up some fliers to post and then check the pound and animal shelters."

"Oh, please find him. I miss my Tricki so much."

Roger said, "He seems like a son to you."

"Better than a son. Always loyal. Always a joy to be around. Please return him to me."

"I know how much he means to you. I'll do my best."

He sat only for a moment before getting up. "Gotta go. We're burnin' daylight."

Mrs. Porcher watched him walk away. He soon disappeared into the woods.

Oh, how she hoped Roger would find Tricki Woo. What would she ever do without him? She didn't want to think about that.

Chapter 7

Roger looked all over the sandy ridge for the missing dog but found nothing. He saw several piles of scat, but none that came from a small dog. One pile a raccoon had left. It contained lots of seeds from a palm tree. Another pile was from a large dog. He noted human footprints. Someone, probably a female from the size of the footprints, used the area for a dog walk, he guessed. Maybe she's seen Tricki Woo if he could find out who exactly she was.

The old orange grove had been let go and was pretty overgrown. This sandy ridge would probably go the way of so many areas like it in Florida. In the near future, it would be full of expensive upscale housing, but today it was the home of neglected orange trees, greenbrier thickets, and scraggly cabbage palms. He made the mistake of brushing against a small hairy plant with nondescript flowers and quickly realized it was the stinging nettle Bill Kenney had warned him about sometime earlier. He pulled some oranges from a tree, cut one open, and tried to rub the hurt away. This did a little good, but not much. He sat down on a fallen oak tree and ate two oranges from two different trees that looked to be of different varieties. Both were good, but the second was sweeter.

He sighed. "Well, dog, where are you?" But the answer eluded him.

Roger decided on a plan of action. He'd do a quick search of the area. With luck, he'd find some evidence of Tricki Woo's passing through. He rounded a bramble patch and startled a gopher turtle. It hissed as it pulled back into its shell and then retreated into its hole, but his head was still visible.

"Sorry about that, Mr. Turtle, that is, assuming you are a mister. Hope you didn't take offense. You do seem to have tough skin. Just the same, sorry." Roger paused and watched the reptile, who likewise was watching him. "You haven't seen a little dog who goes by the name of Tricki Woo, have you?"

The turtle just stared at Roger. "Okay, I see you're the silent type. I'm no Doctor Dolittle. I've still got a long way to go before I can talk to the animals."

The turtle continued to stare. "Guess you're the strong, silent type. I better get back to my search." Roger turned quickly, and the turtle disappeared back into the hole. Roger grunted, "Guess I got a long way to go before I can be like Doctor Dolittle."

Roger looked around some more. He tried to move quietly so as not to surprise any more animals and not to come in contact with anything more that would sting him, plantwise or animal. He saw bees streaming in and out of a hollow tree and wondered if there were any snakes in there. It looked like a good place for them, especially rattlers. He stopped for a moment and an armadillo almost walked into him before stopping. It hesitated, seeming not sure what to do. Roger stomped his foot, and the armored creature jumped straight up. It hit the ground running and was soon gone. Roger'd heard they had terrible eyesight and could jump and run like the dickens, but this was the first time he'd seen it for himself.

He searched some more, but still saw no evidence of Tricki Woo or his passing through. Roger found his way back to sandy Oakwood Avenue and headed down the slope to Mrs. Porcher's and where his truck was parked.

A woman with a dog on a leash came out of a house and hailed him. "Excuse me. Are you looking for something? I saw you in the woods."

Roger stopped. "Why, yes, I am. A lost dog."

"Tricki Woo?"

"Yes. How did you know?"

She smiled. "Lucky guess. It's hard to keep a secret in this neighborhood." She walked over to Roger as the large dog pulled her along. He sniffed at Roger when he got there. "Stop, Bruno. How many times have I told you that's not polite?" She pulled the dog back. "Sorry, she looks frightening, but she loves people. So sorry."

"That's alright. I know enough about dogs to know that one waggin' his tail is usually friendly. My name's Roger Pyles, and yes, I'm looking for Tricki Woo. Have you seen him?"

"So, he's missing again. Not surprised. He's taken off before but been found very quickly. My name's Betsy Smith. I live here."

"Pleased to meet you, Mrs. Smith."

"Betsy is fine, and I'm back to being a Miss again or maybe a Ms. I'm recently divorced. I got the house and the dog. My ex got the road and the girlfriend. Glad that's over."

"Sorry to hear about your misfortune."

She looked down and said nothing.

Roger said, "You seem to be familiar with Tricki Woo."

She laughed. "Yes, he showed up here pretty regularly. We got Bruno as a pup. Neither my ex nor me knew much about dogs, and we thought she was a male. When she grew up, we found Tricki

Woo in our yard humping her. That's when we figured out Bruno was no boy. She was too young to get pregnant, and we got her fixed soon afterward, but that didn't stop Tricki. He'd show up and try to get her, even though she wasn't interested. Finally, she got so big he couldn't reach her without a ladder, but that never stopped him from showing up and trying. It was almost comical watching."

Roger laughed. "Yeah, I'll bet. So, you haven't seen him here lately?"

She shook her head. "No, not for several days. Mrs. Porcher's man help came around and asked about the dog, and I told him what I told you."

"Seems like a tight neighborhood."

"It is. Everyone knows everyone, and their business, too." She laughed.

Roger looked at her, puzzled. He knew she had more to say. "Something you think might be helpful?"

"Helpful, no. Humorous and amusing, yes."

"Go on"

"After the help is gone for the day, and it gets dark, Mrs. Porcher likes to swim naked in her small pool. She thinks no one sees her, but we do. It's not a pretty sight."

"I can imagine."

"Her son used to, too, when he was younger and lived there. She'd go away for the weekend, and he'd throw some wild parties in her absence. They'd be noisy, but he had the good sense to keep it down and not go on when the neighbors wanted to sleep. They knew not to cross the line and get the cops called on them."

"Now, that is interestin'. Won't help me find Tricki, but it sure was an amusin' surprise."

Betsy said, "Like I said, secrets are hard to keep in this cozy little neighborhood. Sorry, I couldn't help you more. My dog's getting antsy. Needs a walk. I better get going. Good luck with finding Tricki."

Roger said, "Thanks, and thanks for the info. Maybe we'll meet again."

She smiled. "I think I'd like that." She stopped. "Has anyone ever told you you resemble Sam Elliott?"

He smiled. "All the time. It's got me in some interestin' situations."

She chuckled. "I can imagine. Got to go, Roger. Bye."

"Bye."

Roger watched as she walked up Oakwood Avenue. *Oh, the wonder of creation. Nothin' like the rise and fall of the female derriere.* He turned away and walked down to his truck. He wasn't much further along in his search for Tricki, but he thought he knew his next place of inquiry, Doctor Solomon, Tricki's vet. Maybe he could be helpful.

Chapter 8

Roger informed Mrs. Porcher he'd found no sign of Tricki Woo. She was relieved that he hadn't found his remains and hopeful he would still turn up. She was rather forceful with her direction for Roger to get on with the search. Time was of the essence. Tricki must be found without delay.

Roger understood her desire to get him back, but was put off by her demanding nature. She didn't like taking no for an answer.

He grumbled to himself as he drove to Doctor Solomon's office on Brevard Avenue in nearby Cocoa. *She's beginnin' to get under my skin. I'm gettin' to have second thoughts about takin' this job for a stubborn old dame.* Still he thought about Tricki Woo. He needed to be found and returned, dead or alive, to the lady that loved him. He hoped for a happy ending.

He saw a small sign that read, Doctor Solomon, Veterinarian, on an old building that looked looked like it had once been a service station. He pulled into the parking area and walked to the building. The door was locked. He pushed a button to an intercom. A voice responded, "Who's there? State your business."

"Roger Pyles. Mrs. Porcher told me you were Tricki Woo's vet, and I needed to talk to you."

After a momentary pause, Roger heard a buzz as the door unlocked. "Come in. Third door to the right."

He went in the semi-lit building. A light came from the third room on the right. Roger popped his head in and said, "Doctor Solomon, I presume."

"Well it ain't Doctor Livingstone. You must be Roger Pyles."

"One and the same. Did I catch you at a bad time?"

"No. Actually, you're in luck. It's a good time, something that's pretty rare for a vet. Usually we're getting a call to pull a foal out of a mare or try to patch up a cat or dog that's been hit by a car. Today's my day for large animal visits. All went well, and I got back early, so I was catching up on some paperwork. Seems like the government's always coming up with another form to simplify my life, but really turns out to be just another burden."

Roger said, "I think President Reagan said it best, 'Government's not the solution, but the problem.'"

"I think he also said, 'If government's the answer, it was a stupid question.'"

Roger laughed.

"So what can I do for you, Roger? What kind of trouble is Tricki Woo in this time?"

"Looks like he took off. Went on walkabout."

"I'm not surprised. He's done that before, but always found his way home after a day or two. How long's he been gone this time?"

"Three or four days, best I can figure out from what Mrs. Porcher has told me."

"That's not good. A lot of things could have happened to him, most of them bad. What's your involvement in this?"

Roger said, "Somehow, Mrs. Porcher found out I have investigative skills. She sought me out and asked, somewhat pleaded, for me to find her Tricki Woo."

Doctor Solomon kicked back in his chair and studied Roger carefully. "So are you the Roger Pyles that's been instrumental in solving some cases in the county and the state? I seem to remember seeing that name in the *Florida Today* newspaper."

"Yeah, I'm that Roger Pyles. Mrs. Porcher seems to think I'm the one who can find her Tricki Woo and get him back. I've never had to use my skills to find a lost pet. I hardly know how to begin. Aren't there services or agencies that do that?"

"Unfortunately, there are no pet finder groups I know of. There should be, but aren't. We've got facilities to find criminals and lost people, but none for pets. I'd like to see Tricki found for his sake and Mrs. Porcher's. Usually, when a dog or cat's lost, people put up posters in the area where the animal was lost. Include a picture of Tricki, some basic information, a reward, if applicable, and some contact information like a phone number where you can reached."

Roger said, "Not sure I want every Tom, Dick, and Harry having my phone number."

"Why don't you get one of those cell phones available at the store? That should be sufficient."

"When did they start doing that?"

"Just recently. Don't you think the area where they launch people into space should be on the cutting edge of technology?"

"Yeah, I guess so. I hadn't thought of that. Good idea. Know a good print shop that works fast with reasonable rates?"

Doctor Solomon said, "I get all my work done by Fineline

Printing. They'll treat you right."

"Thanks. Doc, you care to speculate on what could have happened to Tricki? Is he lost? Was he dognapped? Did he take off?"

"It could be any of the above. He's been known to dig under the fence and go roaming. Sometimes he likes to wander, but when the lust hits him, it's hard to tell where he could have gone in pursuit of happiness and fulfillment. Maybe a long ways. He could be a horny little fellow."

Roger smiled. "So I've heard. Dogs will go far to find satisfaction."

"Men, too."

"You aren't kiddin' on that. Many a man has got himself in a pickle by following his lust. Doc, do you think he could have been taken by someone, and if someone, who?"

The doctor rubbed his chin. "It's possible. It's well known the old lady has lots of bucks and loved the dog. Someone could have taken him. Could have been a stranger. Could have been someone close to the family who saw an opportunity."

"Like a son or daughter?"

"Possibly. The daughter doesn't get along with the mother well, but I don't believe she would take Tricki to hurt her mother. Now the son on the other hand, that's a different story. He's...let's see. How should I say this? Somewhat lacking in character."

Roger said, "You mean he's a womanizer with a drinkin' problem who's never worked a day I his life."

"Bingo, you hit the nail on the head, though I believe his

father forced him to do some honest work when he was a young teenager, but I think he's recovered from that brief experience. I see someone has filled you in on him."

"And who told me that in confidence will remain unnamed."

Doc said, "It's best that way. I want to give you a little warning. A poster with reward money offered will bring out the worst in some people. Some will want money for useless information they made up. Some well-meaning people will provide information that's wrong and will lead you on a wild goose chase. And some are outright con artists. You may get a call from someone who says they found Tricki wandering, and they rescued him, thought he was lost. They'll tell you they've now gone home, somewhere up north, and you need to send money so they can get Tricki back to you. Most of the time calls like that are just thieves looking for easy money. Beware if their main concern is the money and not the dog's welfare. A dog like that would attract attention, and people would be more likely to try to help him than they would a run of the mill mutt. It's sad, but true."

Roger sighed. "So what you're sayin' is that just like in police investigations, I have to follow every lead."

"Correct. Like finding a needle in a haystack."

"True. Just gotta figure out how to simplify and speed up the process."

"I can see you've done something like this before."

Roger said, "Several times."

The phone on the desk rang and Doctor Solomon answered. Roger listened. It seemed someone had a bloated horse and needed immediate help. Doc said he'd be right there. He sat the receiver down.

Roger said, "Looks like an emergency, and you need to go."

"Yes. Good luck with your search. Give me a call if I can help you further. Tricki needs to be found."

"Thanks, Doc. I'll do that." He got up. "I can find my own way out. I won't keep you away from your call."

"Thanks, Roger. Good to meet you, and call if I can be of further assistance."

Roger nodded and left. He stopped at a store, bought a cell phone, but it sure wasn't cheap. No worry. Mrs. Porcher would be paying for it. She said to spare no expense. With help from the young store clerk wearing huge earrings, he activated it. He got information from Mrs. Porcher for the poster and gave her the cell phone number. She said to please hurry. She'd die without her Tricki Woo. Roger politely told her he'd do his best and not to worry, but it didn't seem to reassure her.

The print shop said they'd put a rush on the poster. Roger offered to pay premium for expedited service. He drove home and took a quick, badly needed shower to wash the filth off. He knew the Bible says man was created from the dust of the earth. As dirty as he was, he believed he had at least the material on him for half a man.

After emerging from the shower, he realized the clean clothes he wanted were in the basket on the other side of the trailer. He walked over there and heard a voice.

"Hello, Roger. Good to see you."

Gloria Hernandez stood outside grinning with Carlos next to her. Roger grabbed the clothes basket and used it to cover his nakedness.

"Gloria! I wasn't expectin' company."

"No kidding. Get yourself presentable. Roger, we need to talk."

Chapter 9

Roger quickly dressed and went out to greet his guests. They'd found seats and were waiting on him. "So, what brings you here today? You could have called and said you were comin'."

Gloria said, "I did call and left a message on your answering machine. Do you ever check it?"

"I just got home. I've been out for some time and came in all hot and dirty. You caught me just out of the shower."

Gloria laughed. "I was hoping you hadn't gone full-fledged nudist on me."

Roger ignored the cut. "What brings you to my humble abode today?"

"I have a favor to ask. A big favor. I was driving to Brunswick, Georgia today. I'm scheduled to teach a class at a police convention there for most of this week. I had all my ducks in a row, but life happens. Carlos was going to stay with a friend. She has a boy about his age he's friends with, but reality happened. She had a family emergency and had to back out at the last minute. I guess I could back out of my commitment and stay home, but I was hoping you could take Carlos while I'm away."

"What about school?"

"They're on break for the week."

Roger turned to his son who'd been seated quietly. "What about you, Carlos? What do you think about this?"

"If it's okay with Mom, it's okay with me."

Roger looked at Gloria, but her face gave little clue to her thoughts. "I'll do it, but it's been a while since I've been in parent mode, and I'm workin' a case, too."

Roger saw her eyes widen with concern. He said, "It shouldn't be dangerous. I've been asked to find a lost dog. How dangerous can that be?"

"Wow, Dad. You're a pet detective!"

Gloria said, "That's a little out of your usual line of investigation."

"It is, but I needed a break. Industrial strength crime can wear you down. I thought a change of pace might do me some good, and I could bring a little happiness into the world by trying to find a lady's lost pet. I don't think it would hurt if Carlos tagged along with me. What do you think?"

Carlos said, "I want in. I wanna help. Please, Mom, can I, pretty please?"

Roger laughed. "Gloria, how can you turn down a request like that?"

"Yeah, Mom. You said I needed to send more time with my Dad."

Gloria shifted uneasily in her seat. "Well, if you're good with it, Roger, it's a done deal. I was hoping you could help. I had few good options. It seems we're all in agreement. Carlos, you're going to be with your Dad until I get back in about five days. I have a suitcase with his things in it. There should be everything he needs."

Roger said, "If not, I'm sure we can improvise or get something."

"All right, then. Let me get it. Thanks, Roger, you're the best." She got up, gave Carlos a kiss on the cheek, and then one to Roger. She smiled and walked to her car. Roger was surprised by her action, but even more by his reaction. Visions of the lusty time in Las Vegas that resulted in Carlos' conception flashed across his head. He shifted and had to adjust the stirring in his loins. How well he remembered those days of passion.

Gloria returned with the suitcase. "Here we go." She noted Roger's discomfort. "What? Is everything okay?"

"Yeah. It's all good. We'll work in out. Whatever comes up, we'll deal with it."

She said. "I'm sure it will go just fine. Oh, I just got a cell phone, so if you need to reach me, Carlos has the number on an index card in his things. Any last questions before I go?"

Roger said, "No, I think I can manage. Carlos, how about you?"

"We'll do good, Dad. I'll take care of you."

Roger smiled as did Gloria. He said, "I'm sure you will. Gloria, you have a good time and don't worry about nothin'. It will all work out."

"Thanks, Roger. I better go." She gave Carlos a big hug. "You behave yourself."

"Mom, you know me."

"That's why I said that."

Roger thought he saw her discretely wipe away a tear.

She said, "You boys have fun. Bye."

They said bye, too. She walked to her car parked by the road and drove off.

Roger said, "Well, buddy. Looks like it's you and me. What next?"

"I'm hungry."

"Do you like SpaghettiOs?"

"Yeah."

"Then SpaghettiOs it is. We'll heat up a can, and then we'll try to figure out our plans while you're here."

"Okay, Dad."

Roger heated up the SpaghettiOs in a pot. Getting them something to eat was the easy part. What to do with a young boy while trying to work a case, even a dog case, was something he'd never done before. And his dad skills were a little rusty. He hoped it was like riding a bike. He hoped that ability would come back quickly. If not, it could be a long five days.

Chapter 10

"Dad, those SpaghettiOs were pretty good. Do you always use paper plates and plastic spoons?"

"Not always, but most of the time. I'm not much of a housekeeper, of course, this ain't much of a house. I found I tended to let dishes pile up in the sink unwashed, so I went to disposable. Saves time, too. I got some chocolate chip cookies from Publix. Want some?"

"Sure. Can I have two?"

"Sure, Carlos. Take what you want. Just don't make yourself sick from a good thing. Not sure your mom would forgive me."

"Can I give one to K9?"

"No, chocolate's not good for dogs and cats."

"Why?"

"I'm not sure why, but just don't give it to them. It's kind of a mystery to me, too. They can eat things that would make us puke, but not chocolate. Those critters are just made different than we are."

Carlos said, "Kinda like girls?"

"Kinda. They're like us, only different. Their plumbing is somewhat different, and their wiring is, too. It makes them interesting but can drive you nuts. We're stuck with them, so you just have to learn how to live with them best you can. It isn't always easy."

"Is that why I don't always get along with Mom?"

Roger said, "That's part of it. She's your mom and wants the best for you. Plus, she's got experience."

"What's that?"

"She's older and has seen a lot more. You're exposed to a lot of ideas that sound good but often aren't. You have to learn from experience; often other's experiences, both the good and the bad ones. Repeat the good ones that work. And learn from their mistakes, so you don't have to repeat them. Saves a lot of time, frustration, and money. It's one of the most valuable reasons for studyin' history. Almost every stupid idea around today has been tried before and proven disastrous time and time again, but people don't seem to learn. They seem prone to do dumb things over and over again."

"Like feeding chocolate chip cookies to dogs and cats?"

"Yup. That would be a good example. Politics too. Somebody in the past has done it, and it didn't work out well."

"What's politics?"

"Where they tell you a lie that will make you feel good, instead of the truth that could be hard, and you may not like, but need to hear." Roger said.

"That's not very good."

"No, it's not, but that's the way the game's played."

"Dad, you ever done anything dumb?"

"Yeah, I have. Sadly, we all can be slow learners. I remember an old lady from back home who used to say, 'Lord, help me to learn the lesson the first time, so I won't have to repeat it.' I think she had a lot on the ball with that idea, but she was lamenting about how she'd had to repeat some of them."

"What's lament?"

"It's a deep regret about something. There's a whole book in the Bible about laments, and it was written by Solomon, who's said to have been the wisest man who ever lived. If he had laments, I guess we all will and do. I think for him and others he knew the right thing to do and still didn't do it. It's called willfully ignorant. We know what we need to do and don't want to do it."

"Like cleaning up my room?"

"Yeah, that and lots of bigger things, too, Carlos." Roger looked off to the horizon.

Carlos said nothing for a moment. "You have some laments, too?"

Roger returned his gaze to his son. "Yeah, some I can change, and some I can't." He paused. "Now, we have to find you a place to sleep for the night. You know where the bathroom is. If you need a shower, get one."

"I don't think I need one. Mom makes me take them, but she still complains. She says there's enough dirt behind my ears to grow potatoes."

Roger laughed. "Mine used to do the same thing. I think it's a mom thing."

"Sometimes she calls them papas."

"That's Spanish for potatoes. You can skip the shower then if you want to, but I got to clean off a spot for you to sleep. This old trailer has two sets of built-in bunk beds, but I usually use them for storage. Got to clean one off for you. I normally sleep outside on the porch in my La-Z-Boy chair."

"Could you sleep in here tonight, Dad? I'd feel better with you closer."

"Okay, if it makes you feel better. I guess a new place can be kinda scary when it gets dark."

"Thanks."

Roger proceeded to move his stuff from the lower bunk beds to the top ones with Carlos's help, but he probably could have done it quicker by himself.

Roger said, "Now, we both got a place to sleep. K9 will miss me."

"Can't she sleep in here with us?"

"No, it would be better if she was outside. She's a guard dog, you know."

"How about the cat?"

"No, she's an outside kitty used to her freedom. She'd probably tear the place apart trying to get out. Determination and claws can do a lot of damage. And don't even think about the donkey."

"No way. He's got his own place, the shed. I saw it. Lots of hay he can lie down in and sleep."

"Donkey sleeps standing up. It's usually a light sleep. That way, he can respond to any troubles quickly."

"Guess I learned something, Dad," Carlos said.

Roger smiled.

"Why you smiling?"

"I like the sound of that... Dad. I thought I'd never hear those words again." Roger felt a tear come to his eye. He wiped it away.

"What's wrong?"

"Nothin'. Think I got a gnat in my eye." He wiped again and smiled. "There. It's all better."

Carlos asked, "What are we going to do tomorrow?"

"Well, the plan is to look for Mrs. Porcher's lost dog. The posters should be ready early tomorrow, and I need to check the local animal shelters to see if he's been picked up, and there're several other places worth stoppin' at. I need to do more lookin' around the area where he disappeared. Maybe even expand the search. You good with that?"

"Sounds like fun working together."

Roger said, "Oh, I know it will be a learnin' experience for both of us. That I guarantee."

The rest of the evening went by quickly. They talked some more, and then Carlos read a book he'd brought with him. Roger contemplated his course of action for tomorrow. When it got dark, they went to bed with hope for a good night's sleep. But that's not what happened.

Chapter 11

"Dad, wake up! Something's happening outside. Sounds like fighting."

"Huh? What? What's goin' on?"

"Something's fighting outside."

It only took a second or two for Roger to go from sound asleep to wide awake.

"Get your clothes on. We'll see what's goin' on."

They quickly dressed. Roger grabbed a flashlight and a ball bat. He hit the porch light, and they were out the door. Roger shined the light around and found Donkey standing next to K9 lying on the ground. She was bloody. Donkey had blood on his hooves and mouth.

"Donkey, did you do that? Shame on you. Why did you do that?"

Donkey nudged K9 with his head. She whined.

"Dad! Look over there," Carlos said and pointed to the edge of the light from the flashlight. "What's that?"

Roger shined the light to where he pointed. A bloody mass of fur lay on the ground.

"What is that, Dad?"

Roger held the bat ready. He wasn't sure if he needed it for Donkey. Cautiously, he approached the bloody heap. "Why, it looks like what's left of a coyote. I think I got this wrong, Carlos. I think K9 was attacked by a coyote, and Donkey came to her rescue. He was tryin' to protect her, not harm her."

"How bad is she hurt?"

"I don't know. We need to find out." They rushed to K9. "Careful, Carlos. Let me take care of this. She's hurt and frightened. She may try to bite us when we try to help her." He went closer. "Easy, girl, easy. Your attacker's dead. The coyote won't hurt you anymore."

K9 whined.

"It's okay. It's okay. Let me see how bad you're hurt." Roger petted her head and worked his way down her back and body. She winced. "Easy, girl, easy."

"How is she, Dad?

"Looks like she got bit several times, but I didn't see anything broken. I'm gonna pick her up and carry her to the porch. I need you to take the light. Open the porch door when I get there."

"Okay, Dad."

Roger stooped to the ground and gently picked up his dog. She cried out.

"Easy, girl. I know this hurts. I'm tryin' to help. We'll get you fixed up."

They walked to the porch. Carlos opened the door, and Roger walked in. Carefully, he laid K9 on her bed. She winced.

"Easy, girl, easy."

Roger examined her more closely. "Don't look too bad. Mainly bites. Could have been a lot worse if Donkey hadn't been around."

"Dad, he's just outside looking at K9."

Donkey stared at the dog and cooed.

Roger said, "Donkey, I owe you an apology. You're the hero here. If not for you, that coyote would have got the best of her. Good Donkey."

He continued to coo.

"Keep an eye on her. I'll get some peroxide inside and treat her wounds."

"Sure."

Roger went inside and quickly returned with the medicine. He poured some on her wounds that fizzed.

"Is that bad, Dad? Should it be doing that?"

"Pretty normal. She doesn't look too bad. The coyote could have done a lot of damage if Donkey hadn't gotten there. I think I'm gonna sleep out here on the porch and keep an eye on her. I'll take her to the vet tomorrow for a more thorough exam. In the meantime, I'll watch her for any signs of real damage I could have missed. You be okay in the trailer by yourself? I'll be right outside on the porch."

"I'd rather you be inside, but I'll do it for K9."

"Good. Try to get some sleep."

"Will do, Dad." He stroked K9's head. "You take care, girl. I'll say some prayers for you." He went inside. Soon, the interior light was extinguished.

Roger stroked the dog's head. "Hang in there. I'm taking you to the vet tomorrow. Hang in there."

She made a pitiful sound.

"I know it hurts. We'll get through this."

Roger stroked her head some more. She closed her eyes.

"Good dog. Glad it's the coyote that's lying in a heap, not you."

He shut the porch light off and lay down in his La-Z-Boy chair. This wasn't how he wanted to start his first day with his son, but life happens. He'd be at Doc Solomon's office when it opened in the morning and get K9 fixed up. Roger hoped she wasn't hurt worse than he thought. These things sure could change his plans for tomorrow. Blessed are the flexible for they shall not be broken.

Chapter 12

Roger reclined in his La-Z-Boy chair on the old trailer's screened-in porch. So much had changed for him recently. After trying to drink himself to death and escape the pain in his heart, he now had some reason to live. There still was a hole in his heart that mourned for his late wife and young son. They say time heals all wounds, but he wasn't sure that was true. It may lessen the pain, but the scars remain to remind him of what had happened.

And now he had Carlos. A few months ago, he hadn't even known he existed. Funny how fate, or was it something greater, moves just when we needed it to. Roger'd felt so alone and lost in this world after losing his professorship at the college and then his wife and son. What a surprise it had been to discover he had another son. His heart had leaped with joy. And then he'd almost lost him when he was hit by the truck. He remembered looking at Carlos when he lay unconscious in the hospital bed, unsure if he would live or die. How Roger wished he could switch places with him. Gladly, he was willing to die in his place if the young boy could live. He guessed that's what love is. He sighed. So much had changed. With this and his work, he had a reason to live. Maybe things would work out. Life could be like a rose garden. You had flowers, but you had thorns, too. A garden must be properly cared for and maintained if you expected flowers and fruits.

K9 whined in her restless sleep.

"Good girl. You're a good girl. Hold on. I'll get you to the doctor first thing in the morning. Hang on. It'll get better. Just got to tough it through the night. Good girl."

K9 open her eyes a little, whined, and closed them. Her breathing became slower, and she drifted off to sleep.

"Good girl," Roger whispered. "Good girl."

This was sure an unpleasant surprise tonight. K9 gettin' in a fight with a coyote. And I thought Donkey was the bad guy. Sure glad Carlos saw the dead coyote. And what of Carlos? I have a case to investigate, even if it is only tryin' to find a lost dog. But still, it is a case. How am I gonna work it with him around? And now, K9's hurt. Guess I'll muddle through it somehow. Gonna have to. But it's good to have him around. Get to know him. Feel like a real father again. That was a good feelin'. I really wondered if I would even know that feelin' again. Roger smiled. *It'll all work out. Tryin' to make it work's half the battle.* And he knew how to work. He closed his eyes and drifted off to sleep.

***

This is turning out different than I expected. I thought me and Ralph would be playing in his yard at his house off Tropical Trail. It's a lot nicer than here, but Ralphie ain't my dad. It was really a surprise when Mom told me who my dad was. I always wanted a real dad. Mom's ex, who I thought was my dad, was never around. That was kind of a real downer. Roger, my daddy, seems like a really neat guy. His place is kind of dumpy and rundown, but I guess he's happy with it just the way it is, so that's okay. It feels kind of homey. Guess that's what's important. Hope Mom had a safe trip to her meetings, and they go okay. Glad Dad said yes when she asked him if it was alright for me to stay with him for the week. He even seemed eager to have me. Carlos smiled. *It's good to be wanted. Even though he barely knows me, I think he loves me. I want to love him. I want a real dad. I want a real family.* He sighed. *Sure wish K9 hadn't gotten hurt. Dad tried to fix her up best he could. Hope she makes it through the night. Dad must think a lot of her staying out there with her. Wish he was in here with me, but you can't be in two places at once.* He sighed again. *Sure is hot in here, even with all the windows open.*

He rolled over on his side. *Dear God, I don't know much about praying. Mom usually has me say the Lay Me Down to Sleep prayer at bedtime, so I'm making this up as I go. Dear God, I know Mom believes in You, even though she sometimes says bad words and then asks for forgiveness. She thinks I don't hear, but I do. She means well and has a lot on her mind. Oh yeah, what I wanted to ask. Could You help K9 get better? I don't know if it's right to pray for a dog, but I didn't think You'd mind if I asked. Do You? I don't want to bother You with little things like a hurt dog when You're so busy holding the world together. So, please help K9 get better, and help Dad find the missing dog. Now, I think I better try to get some more sleep. So, now I lay me down to sleep. I pay the Lord my soul to keep. If I should die before I wake, I pray the Lord my soul to take. Amen.*

Carlos rolled over on his other side. He wondered about tomorrow and hoped all went well. Soon he was fast asleep and Donkey stood guard outside against any threats, real or imagined.

Chapter 13

It was barely daylight when Roger woke up. Donkey stood in the yard about 25 feet away from the trailer. He snored softly. Roger got up from the La-Z-Boy chair. The noise woke Donkey, and he trotted over to the porch and looked at K9. She still slept on her mat.

"Good dog. Good dog." Roger carefully stroked her head and examined her in the dim light. She stirred and whimpered. Donkey made some soft cooing sounds. "Yeah, Donkey, we're all worried about her. I'm taking her to the vet when he opens up."

Donkey cooed again, stared intensely at K9, turned, and then wandered off grazing as he went. He stopped at the dead coyote and then continued his walk and grazing. Roger filled K9's water and food bowl. She got up with effort, lapped at the water, and laid back down. She moaned.

"Hold on, girl. Ole Doc Solomon knows a thing or two about fixin' you up. In a few days, you'll be as good as new. You'll heal up, but it will take a little time. Hang in there."

She sighed and closed her eyes.

Roger went into the trailer and saw Carlos was still sleeping. He searched through the small refrigerator and mumbled to himself. "There has to be something in here to eat besides beer." Behind several six-packs, he found an egg carton with three eggs in it. They seemed good. The half-eaten pack of bologna smelled okay, too. He found a partial loaf of bread and discarded about half that had mold on it, green like penicillin. A pack of strawberry jelly and another of butter he'd gotten at a restaurant sometime in the distant past would go on the bread. And an unopened bottle of Florida's Finest Orange Juice would round out the meal. The expiration date said it was a month out of date, but it smelled good. He knew he had two packets of ketchup on the table. *That'll get us through breakfast. Looks like I'll need a trip to the store to keep us from starvin'.*

He heard a voice behind him. "Dad, I'm sorry. I think I wet the bed."

Roger turned and saw that Carlos's pants were wet in the front. He tried to put his best foot forward. "It's okay. Get yourself some clean and dry clothes. Drop them on the floor, and I'll take care of them. You'll need a shower to clean up."

"Okay. That's what mom has me do when I have an accident." He paused. "What's for breakfast?"

"Good stuff. It'll be a surprise. I'll have it done when you're done and presentable."

"Okay, Dad." He turned, grabbed some clothes from the suitcase, and disappeared into the bathroom.

Roger had enough food in the refrigerator to whoop up a breakfast, a surprise to him. His luck had prevailed, but a wet bed, that was another surprise, an unpleasant one. Poor kid. That had to be embarrassing, he was sure of that. He remembered growing up and having waterworks at night. The old country doctor said he'd outgrow it back then. He did, but not near soon enough for his mom or him, either. It was a frustrating time for both of them. Roger remembered it all too well. Carlos truly was his father's son.

Roger fried the eggs and bologna. He put two slices of bread in the toaster and found two plastic cups for the juice. When all was ready, he put it on paper plates and got out two packets of plastic ware complete with salt and pepper and a napkin.

"Carlos, breakfast is ready," Roger yelled.

"Be there in a jiffy."

About a minute later, he came out of the bathroom and walked to the other end of the trailer. His hair was wet and disheveled. "Smells good. I'm hungry. What is it?"

"Eggs, toast with condiments, fried bologna, and orange juice. Dig in. I forgot to make some coffee. My mind must have been someplace else." He got up and got Mr. Coffee perking.

"This fried bologna is pretty good. I never had it fried before."

Roger said, "My mom used to serve it up to us when I was little. It's kind of a thing up in the Appalachian Mountains where I grew up."

"It's pretty good." He dropped his eyes. "Sorry about the bed."

"It's okay. I had the same problem growin' up. You'll outgrow it. I did."

"I hope so. The doctor mom takes me to says the same thing."

Roger asked, "Did you sleep well?"

"It was hot, and the bed was lumpy. A mouse ran out of it."

"What? A mouse ran out of the mattress?"

Carlos said, "Just a little one. Food's good, Dad."

"It tastes better when you're hungry. So, a mouse was livin' in the mattress. We need to get rid of it. Better check the others for mice, too. Sounds like I need to get some traps. Looks like the cat's been slackin'."

"Dad, we keep talking, and the food will get cold."

"Good point. Let's eat."

The hungry boys wolfed the food down. When they finished, Roger disposed of the plates but rinsed out the cups for future use. Roger noted a buzzing sound.

"Going to answer your phone, Dad?"

"Oh yeah, not used to havin' one you can carry around. Wonder who it can be?" He pulled it out of his pocket. "Hello? Why, Mrs. Porcher. What a surprise. No, I haven't found Tricki Woo. I just got up. Gotta go to the vets as soon as he opens. My dog got in a fight with a coyote last night. Yes, that is terrible. Thank you for your concern. Yes, I will be puttin' up posters and looking for Tricki after I'm done at Doctor Solomons. Yes, I think he's a good vet, too. Thank you. Let's keep our fingers crossed and hope we find Tricki today. Goodbye Mrs. Porcher."

Carlos asked, "Who was that?"

"Mrs. Porcher. I'm lookin' for her dog, Tricki Woo. He's a Pekingese"

"A Pekingese?"

"Little hairy dog with lots of spirit. I hope she doesn't call me all the time." He stopped. "We need to go. Carlos, here are my keys. I'll get K9, and you unlock the truck."

"Sure." The young boy exited the trailer. "Look. She's standing up."

Roger said, "That's a good sign. I'll pick her up and carry her to the truck. You keep her comfortable while I drive to the vet."

"Sure thing, Dad."

Roger carefully picked up K9. She winced. "Easy girl. We're goin' to get you help. Stay with me. We have to tough it out."

He carried her to the truck. The doors were open, and he placed her at Carlos's feet. The boy stroked her head. "It will be alright."

Roger took the keys, drove to the gate, opened and closed it without Donkey eloping, and drove toward Cocoa. He sure hoped his happy talk about K9 going to be okay would come true. The doc had to have something that would be magic cure. He hoped.

Chapter 14

Roger drove slowly down the washboard unpaved road laughingly known as Canaveral Flats Boulevard. K9 still winced when he hit a bad rut. Carlos spoke gently to her and stroked her chin and head. He said, "Good girl. You're a good girl."

She wagged her tail weakly.

"That's a good sign," Roger said.

"What is?"

"She's feeling well enough to wag her tail, even if it is somewhat feeble. She wasn't doin' that last night after the fight."

Carlos smiled but said nothing as he continued to run his hand over K9's head. Traffic was heavy on US 1, and there was a fender bender at the intersection with the Beeline Expressway. Two Cocoa city police cars with lights flashing sat blocking off the crash. One cop was directing traffic while the other was filling out a report. Two groups of people with concerned faces stood on the nearby sidewalk as a tow truck loaded one of the damaged cars onto it. A half a mile later, they took a left on Brevard Avenue and about a thousand feet later, took another left into the parking lot of the vet's office, an old service station from the outward looks of it.

The sign on the door said the office hours today were 8 to 5. It was a little before 8, but Roger tried the door anyway, but found it locked. He walked to where Carlos sat in the truck with K9. "I'm goin' around the back. Maybe the doc is in and he'll open up for us."

"Okay."

Roger disappeared around the back, and a few minutes later, the front door opened. He exited, and Carlos could see an older man in a white coat with gray hair behind him in the building. He could hear dogs yelping from somewhere in the building. Roger walked to the truck. "Doc Solomon said to bring K9 in. You hop out and I'll carry her in. Open the office door for me, okay?"

"Sure thing."

All went as planned. Doc Solomon was waiting for them in the reception room. He said, "Take her to the next room, and I'll take a look at her. See how bad she's hurt. Does she bite?"

Roger sat her on the stainless steel table. "Probably not, but you know how hurt animals, two or four-legged, will strike out."

The vet nodded knowingly. "How true that is." He put his hand forward carefully and scratched her chin. "Good girl. Let's see what that bad old coyote did to you." He inspected her carefully from nose to tail and all parts in between. "She's got a bunch of bite marks. The worst seems to be around her neck. Seems the coyote was going in for the kill. You say your donkey killed the coyote? They usually don't interfere in fights like this. They don't like either dogs or coyotes and if one kills the other, so be it."

Roger said, "Yeah, the donkey killed the coyote. Stomped and bit him to death."

"Most unusual. She'll recover with time. I'll give her a shot with some pain killer, antibiotics, and vitamins in it to lessen the pain and help her heal up. I'd say within two or three weeks, she should be back to her old self, good as new."

"That's good to hear, Doc."

Carlos said, "Yippy."

"And who is this young man with you, Roger?"

"This is my son, Carlos."

The doctor said, "Good to meet you, young fellow." He turned to Roger. "You'll want to keep an eye on her. No strenuous activities and if she doesn't seem to be improving, bring her back. I'm worried about infection. I can give you some sample vitamins and drugs a salesman gave me. It'll save you some money."

"Thanks Doc. What do I owe you?"

The doctor told him, and Roger paid with cash. "Thanks, Doc, for openin' early and seein' us."

"Emergencies seem to happen at the most inconvenient times."

"Very true. Now, I best be goin'. I got a lot to do today. Thanks again. Oh, anythin' more you can tell me about Mrs. Porcher and Tricki Woo?"

"She's a little eccentric and used to getting her way. When she got to calling me Uncle Herriot like in the TV show, I had to draw the line at that. It was Doctor Solomon, but I did accept the sherry and biscuits she gave me, just like Mrs. Pumphrey did in the series. And she loves her Tricki Woo, often too much. She spoils him with rich food that's not good for him. A while back, I had to take him in to recover from her pampering. Too much people food was killing him. He was very overweight and sick. Even had flop bott."

"Flop bott? Can't say I ever heard of that condition," Roger said.

"Flop bott is indicted when a dog drags his butt across the ground because his anal glands are clogged. That was what she called it. I have to purge them regularly because of the people food she spoiled him with."

"So, how do you treat flop bott?"

"It's pretty easy. You squeeze on both sides of the anus until the discharge comes out. Or you can do it internal, You…"

"I get the picture, doc."

"Dealing with all God's creatures, great and small, can be earthy."

"And that includes humans?"

"Most certainly, but I leave that to the MDs. Sometime I prefer dealing with animals over humans."

Roger said, "I can understand that completely."

"Now back to when Tricki Woo stayed with me at the office. Two weeks of standard dog food and just running around here with the other dogs did him wonders. Tricki is a dog and likes doing dog things. And he's a true Pekingese. Loyal, affectionate, intelligent, strong-willed, has that distinctive walk, and makes a good guard dog. He killed a rat that somehow found its way into my building. Good breeding, too. Wide and open nostrils. Some Pekingese dogs had trouble breathing because of the flat face. He's all dog, and Mrs. Porcher seems to forget that, just like the old grand dame in the English show."

Roger said, "You think he might have run off to do some of those dog things?"

"Very possible. He does seem to have a streak of lust in him. I told her I could take care of that, but Mrs. Porcher wouldn't hear of it." He paused. "Have you picked up the missing dog posters yet?"

"No. I'll do that this mornin' after I get K9 home."

"Travis Hardware's a good place for all your needs. It's at the corner of 520 and Delannoy Street. The owner, Mack's a friend of mine. You do have a stapler to put them up?"

"I remember seeing it on the way to Merritt Island. Guess I'll have one when I get it at Travis's. Got a big selection?"

"Everything in the hardware line you can image or your heart would desire."

"That's good to know. Thanks, Doc."

They took K9 to the truck. She only whimpered once on the way back to the trailer. The painkillers seem to have kicked in. Once there, Roger laid her on her bed. She went to sleep quickly.

Roger said, "Poor little girl. All tuckered out." His cell phone rang, and he answered. "Hello. Mrs. Porcher, what a surprise. No. No new news on Tricki Woo. I just got back from the vet's office with my dog. What? I'm losin' you. What?" The phone went dead. "Guess I lost her."

Carlos said, "Can I see the phone, Dad?" He handed the phone to him. "You forgot to charge it. The battery's dead."

"Charge it? How often do you have to do that?"

"Every day, especially a new phone that probably didn't get a good first charge."

73

Roger said, "How do you know so much about them things?"

"Mom got me one. She calls me to check on me, but I ignore about half her calls. Mothers can be a pain, always wanting to know what I'm doing. Don't tell her I told you that."

"Your secret's good with me. Now, I'd like you to stay with K9 today. Someone needs to keep an eye on her. I'll get your cell phone number and call from a payphone when I'm down there lookin' for Tricki."

"Okay. I'll do that. Will you be back for lunch?"

"I don't think so. I know I have more SpaghettiOs, and there's something in the refrigerator. Look around. You'll find something I'm sure to fill your tummy."

"Okay, Dad."

"And I want to fix things up for you. I'm gonna get Lester to put a window unit air conditioner in the trailer to cool you down, and you can sleep better."

"Thanks. Who's Lester?"

"Lester's a handyman and a good friend of mine. Look for an old black man to show up this mornin'. That would be Lester. Just stay out of his way and let him work. He's a good guy."

"Sure thing. I won't let you down."

They talked a little more. Roger called Lester and made arrangements for the work. After giving Carlos a hug and checking on K9, he drove off in his truck. He had much to do. He hoped all went well today. It seemed like a simple job, find a lost dog. He hoped it was as easy as it sounded. What could go wrong?

Chapter 15

"Uh-oh." Flashing blue lights in the distance got Roger's attention. A patrol car blocked US 1 about a half-mile south of Canaveral Flats Boulevard. Roger muttered to himself. "Could have been me if I'd been a little earlier."

He went straight across US 1 over to River Road and then took a right. "Looks like it's the scenic route today." He liked the old houses from the past and noticed several new, modern-style homes that were generally bigger and more ornate. There were very few houses on the riverside. The burned-out remains of one that exploded some time ago stood out like a sore thumb. A gas leak was the official story. He figured when the investigation was over and a clear title was available, someone would snatch up the choice property and rebuild on it, but now it was a blackened pile of rubble, wood, and debris.

Several more miles of narrow, twisty roadway passed, and he stopped at Route 520. A couple of turns and he pulled into the parking lot at Travis Hardware. He got out and walked a block to the print shop. Yes, they had the posters done. They exceeded Roger's expectations, and he was more than happy to pay the extra charge for the expedited work. Traffic was heavy on the eastbound street to Merritt Island. He crossed the busy road when the light changed, creating a lull. Roger walked into the back of the store. It looked like it had been around a hundred years which it had.

75

"Can we help you?" a male voice said.

Roger saw a large man with a beard sitting on a stool, and he was smiling.

"Can we help you, young man? We're here to meet all your hardware needs and more. We got old stuff, new stuff, and everything in between, and if by chance, which is very unlikely, we don't have it, we can and will get it for you." He stuck out his hand. "Name's Mack. I own this place. It's been in my family since its beginning."

Roger shook his hand and looked around. "Yeah, you have quite a selection. I'm in need of a stapler. I'm Roger Pyles."

Got a bunch of them on the second floor. Delly, would you take him up there and show him our inventory?"

"Sure boss," an attractive woman of about thirty-five years of age said. "Follow me, Mr. Pyles."

"Okay, but make it Roger."

She smiled. "Sure thing, Roger. Follow me."

She climbed the stairs that turned twice to the second floor. Roger noted and liked the tight-fitting jeans in front of him at eye level. At the top of the stairs, she turned and saw him gazing. She grinned as he did as well.

"Follow me."

"Lead me on."

She went down one aisle, zigzagged, and down another aisle to the end, where the staplers were.

"Man, you got all kinds. I never knew there were so many."

"We have manual, electric, and pneumatic, everything from ones used in an office to heavy-duty industry. Surely, we have something that meets your needs. What were you planning on nailing?"

"I need to put up some posters."

"I'd recommend a manual, either a hammer tacker or this heavy-duty staple gun." She picked them up and handed them to Roger.

"I like the feel of this one, the hammer tacker. I can just put the poster on the pole, whack it with this four times, and be done. Right?"

She smiled. "You got it, Roger."

He looked at the price tag. "Reasonable, too."

"Most people are surprised at our prices. We try to give our customers real value."

Roger nodded and noted her extended look at him. "What? Did I say something funny?"

"No. Is your name really Roger Pyles? You look like that movie star."

"I hear that all the time."

"You sure look like Tom Selleck."

"Don't you mean Sam Elliott? They were in a lot of movies together?"

She grinned. "I believe you're right."

"It's got me in a lot of trouble. I had a woman try to put the moves on me, and my late wife was standing right there with me."

"So what happened?"

"Kay sent her packin'. Told her I was taken and if she wanted meat, go to a butcher shop. It was kind of funny later."

"You said late wife?"

"She died in an auto accident." He lowered his eyes.

"I'm sorry," she said. "I didn't mean to cause you discomfort."

"It's okay," he said. "Tell me, is Delly your full name, or is it short for something else?"

"It's Delilah."

He smiled, "My, my, my, Delilah."

"You'll never know how many times I've heard that since Tom Jones sang the song."

"Well, Delilah, you can meet all my hardware needs." He grinned, as did she. "Here." He handed her a poster. "You can reach me at the phone number on the poster if you like. And if you would, please post the notice. I'm lookin' for a lost dog."

She glanced at the notice. "Why, that's Tricki Woo. Mrs. Porcher comes in regularly and gets a special dog food for him that only Mack can get. I've loaded it in the back of her gold Rolls."

"That's Mrs. Porcher, alright."

"I'll have Mack put it up. Let's get you checked out." She handed him a business card. "It's got my phone number on it. Maybe we could get together and get to know each other better."

Roger smiled. "Sounds good to me. We better get downstairs. I've got a dog to find."

"Sure thing."

Roger followed, and he was sure there was some extra wiggle in her hips as she went down the stairs.

"There they are. Land sakes. I thought I was going to have to get up a search party and come look for you," Mack said.

Roger said, "It took a while for me to decide which one I wanted, but she showed me the whole selection."

Mack said, "I'll bet she did." He gave her a dirty look. She looked away.

"I'll take this one." Roger handed him a twenty.

Mack made the change and gave him a receipt. "That's a good one, you got there. Got a thirty-day guarantee. Bring it back if you have any troubles."

"Thanks."

Delly said, "Boss, Tricki Woo has run away. Roger's trying to find him. He asked if we could put up this poster." She handed it to Mack.

He took a quick look. "Sure thing. Hope you find what you want." His eyes went to Delly again and back to Roger. He smiled the whole time.

"Thanks, Mack. Your store had a lot of surprises."

"Ain't that a fact? Come back again. You're a stranger only once."

"Sure thing."

Roger walked out the back door and sat down in his truck. *That woman could sure rev up my motor.* He worked his way through Cocoa Village along the Indian River and south into Rockledge. He turned onto Oakwood Street and pulled into Mrs. Porcher's driveway. He no more than turned off the ignition when she came out of the house with a cloth in her hand. Tears ran down her cheeks.

"Oh, it's dreadful, Roger, absolutely dreadful."

"What's wrong? Tell me, please."

Chapter 16

"They've found Tricki Woo. He's dead."

"What happened?"

Mrs. Porcher wiped away a tear. "They found him dead in the road. He'd been hit."

She sniffed.

"Who're they?" Roger asked.

"I have some friends in the Rockledge Police. One of them, Lt. Nyquist, found him lying in the middle of Barton Boulevard, the busy part west of US 1. This is dreadful. What shall I do? How can I live without my Tricki Woo?" She began to cry and place her head on Roger's shoulder.

He held her as the tears flowed. What could he do? Not much, so he tried to comfort her the best he could. He heard a car approaching, a black and white Rockledge City Police four-door sedan, a Ford Crown Vic, he thought. "Mrs. Porcher, let me take care of this. You need to sit down."

She looked up at him through her teary eyes and nodded. "Perhaps you're right. This is so traumatic. Please, help me."

Roger presented his arm and walked her to the chair by the pool.

"Thank you," she said as she wiped away a tear.

He nodded and walked to the police car. The officer stood outside. He had a grim look on his face. Roger said, "Are you here about the dog?"

"I am. I have him in the trunk."

"I'm Roger Pyles. Mrs. Porcher asked me to find him. She's not takin' this too well and wants me to check out the body."

"I understand." He popped the trunk open. "Take a look."

It was definitely a Pekingese and definitely dead. The small dog lay on its side with a black tongue lolling out of its mouth. And it definitely resembled the picture he had of Tricki Woo.

"Poor little fella," the cop said in a whisper so Mrs. Porcher couldn't hear. "He was lying along the side of the road so peaceful you would have thought he was sleeping. I stopped and checked on him. Definitely dead. Must have gotten hit early this morning. He wasn't all broken up like some I've seen. Must have been hit by the underside of the vehicle."

Roger carefully checked out the little broken body. He too whispered. "Yeah, I think you're right. His neck's broken and so are some of his ribs. If there's a good point to this, he didn't suffer. Sure does look like the picture I was given to find Tricki."

"Are you the same Roger Pyles that's been tracking down criminals in the area? I thought you looked familiar. Saw an article in the local paper you were mentioned in and it had your picture."

"That's me. Got to roll him over. There. Hmm. Do you see what I see?"

"What do you see?"

"This dog sure looks like Tricki. He's colored the same, but this isn't Mrs. Porcher's dog. This dog's been neutered, and her dog hasn't been. It's a beautiful dog, but it's not Tricki Woo. Someone else is missin' their little dog."

Officer Nyquist said, "I'll leave it to you to break the news to her."

"Okay. I'll tell her." Roger walked over to her. She wiped away another tear. "Mrs. Porcher, I've got good news and bad news."

"I know the bad news. He's dead. What's the good news?"

"He looks like Tricki Woo, but it's not your dog. The dog in the car's been neutered, and Tricki had all his equipment intact."

Her face brightened. "Oh, that's wonderful. There's still hope." And then it sank. "But someone is missing their little companion as much as I am. Do you think you could find the owner? If it was my dog, I'd want to know what happened to him."

"He had no collar or tags, but if he's been chipped, maybe Doctor Solomon could find out."

"Please do that for me and his owner."

"I will." He stopped. "I was goin' to put up the posters the printer made."

"It shouldn't take too long. Doctor Solomon owes me a favor, and I'd like you to take him a bottle of apricot brandy. It's his weak spot."

Roger smiled. *Yeah, she was used to gettin' her way and knows just how to get it.* "If you say so. I'll have Officer Nyquist put the body in the back of my truck, and I'll drive right to the vets."

"And if you can't find out who owns him, would you bury him up in the old grove? I have shovels in the shed. The ground up there's all sand, and the digging should be easy."

"Yeah, I can do that if need be."

"Very well. Off with you, Roger. There's still hope. You must find my Tricki."

"Okay, Mrs. Porcher. As you noted, we're burnin' daylight."

She wiped the last of the tears from her face and smiled.

Officer Nyquist moved the little dog from his car to the back of Roger's truck, and they both departed. Doctor Solomon was busy but said he would check ASAP, and he gave Roger some paperwork to fill out about K9, and a bill for services he'd forgotten. It took a few minutes to complete the form. He waited a few more minutes, and the doctor appeared with a small device in his hand. "Ready?" the doctor said.

"Yeah, follow me."

They walked outside to the far side of the lot, where Roger parked under a tree.

Doctor Solomon said, "I appreciate you considering others. A dead dog can be unsettling to some. And the shade will slow decomposition." He ran the scanner over the dog's shoulders several times. "Nope. No chip. A collar, but no tags. Definitely a nice dog, and sure does look like Tricki, but I know it's not. This dog has a little white patch on his chest. Tricki Woo didn't have a spot like that." He checked the body. "Seen it all too often. Dog versus motor vehicle. Dog loses. At least it was a quick death from a broken neck. What are you going to do with the body?"

"Mrs. Porcher thought we could bury him in the old grove on the sand hill behind her house."

"That would be good. If you left him here, he'd go in a plastic bag and then the dumpster. I hate to do it, but don't have much choice when people leave their animals here for disposal. I'd spend all my time digging holes for animals and no time for caring for them."

"You don't have to explain yourself to me. I know what has to be done. The details ain't always pretty." Roger reached into his wallet and pulled out two twenties. "Here, that should make us square."

"You overpaid."

"Consider it a tip. A thank you for services above and beyond the usual call of duty."

"Well, thank you. And I hope you find Tricki. Now, I must get back to work. Good luck, Roger."

"Doc, I'm gonna need it."

They parted, and Roger was soon back at Mrs. Porcher's. James helped him find a shovel in the garage. He drove up to the end of sandy Oakwood Street and found a suitable place for a burial. After digging a hole about two and a half feet deep, he gently placed the small dog in the hole. "For a little dog, you sure are heavy. Guess I should say some words. Everyone and everything should be remembered at the end." He looked skyward. "Lord, I'm not much of a prayin' man. Some people say animals don't have souls. That may be true, but I know they'll be in heaven 'cause You said everything your heart could desire will be there, and I know it wouldn't be perfect without our pets. Amen."

He sighed and then began the grim task of filling in the hole. Done, he gazed at the little sand mound. *Such a shame for a noble creature like that to end up like this. At least he had a proper burial, and the buzzards didn't get him.* He sighed again, placed the shovel in the back of the truck, grabbed the stapler and posters, and began putting them up. He had another dog to find and hoped it went better than it had for this little dog. Roger didn't want to give the old lady bad news again. *Lord, help me find Tricki Woo alive, if only for Mrs. Porcher's sake.* He sighed yet again. *Tricki Woo, where are you?*

Chapter 17

Tricki Woo didn't have a care in the world. Well, he did have a few concerns. He missed Mrs. Porcher fussing over him and giving him his tasty treats, and the woman who groomed his hair. The only bad points since the beginning of his adventure had been getting chased by the big dog, but he escaped by crawling under a fence, finding his own food, and a safe place to stay during the night.

All and all, it had been a grand adventure. He'd met many dogs along the way, who, after they sniffed each other's rear ends, wanted to tussle and play. Some even shared their bowls of food with him. And the times he had with the lady dogs. My, oh my. One old lady had caught them in the act and chased him away, but Tricki came back later when she went inside, and they went at it again, this time uninterrupted.

People had been nice to him, but not as nice as Mrs. Porcher. One had even tried to get him in his vehicle, but Tricki ran away. He wanted his freedom. His grand adventure beckoned him on. He had a good idea of where his final destination was, but there was no hurry to get there as long as he could find a way to fill his belly and have fun along the way.

Only one thing had really bothered him along the way-the dog that looked like him and wouldn't move out of the road. He'd heard a yelp, saw the other dog go under the vehicle, and come to rest by the curb. Tricki knew he had to find out what had happened.

The other dog looked like him. He just laid there, not moving with his tongue hanging out. No matter how Tricki licked his face and whimpered encouragement, he didn't move.

He was puzzled about this until he remembered the time when he was a little puppy. All was fine. It had been so much fun playing with his brothers and sisters and his mother, although for some reason, she seemed more interested in nursing them than playing. One day, he woke up and found his mother standing over one of his sisters. She licked her with her long wet tongue and whimpered like he had with the dog in the road, but his sister did not move or respond. The man who watched over them and fed his mother found the still pup and tried to get her to move. After some effort, he shook his head and took his sister away. His mom seemed distressed, and they never saw his sister again. After a day or so, life went back to normal.

Perhaps the same thing had happened to the dog that could be his twin. Maybe a man would come along and take him away, too, just like one had done with his sister. He wasn't sure, but he knew he could do no more for the other little dog, so he went on. A kind man who sat on a plastic bucket behind a BBQ restaurant had shared his lunch with him and removed his collar. Tricki didn't think he needed it and was glad it was gone. The man seemed quite happy after the exchange. Tricki ran off when he tried to grab him. Freedom and the open road called, and he must respond.

He tried to get water in a big ditch, but a big log had snapped at him, but Tricki was fast. He wouldn't make that mistake again, no matter how still and dead the log looked. After he'd scrambled up the bank and out of the log's grasp, he looked at the log again. It had eyes and looked at him menacingly. And legs-four stubby legs, and a tail. After a moment, it hissed and raced into the water. Only its eyes were above the surface, and they burned a hole in Tricki. This was no log, but something else, and Tricki knew it was in his best interest to avoid things of this nature, whatever it was. Adventures could have surprises, most good, but occasionally, a bad one he didn't want to experience again.

Would he go to his original destination or not? Perhaps there would be other adventures calling on his walkabout. You never know what was just around the corner that needed exploring.

Chapter 18

After burying Tricki Woo's doppelganger, Roger posted the missing dog notices around Mrs. Porcher's neighborhood. He checked the rocky ledge along the Indian River from which the town took its name but found nothing but a few empty beverage containers and assorted miscellaneous trash careless people discarded. There was no sign of Tricki.

Mrs. Porcher'd stopped him as he drove by and asked him if he had any progress reports for her. Roger told her what he'd done so far, but no, Tricki Woo was still missing. Her face showed distress. Her makeup had tracks where tears had flowed. He tried gently to tell her he had to get back to work, and her questions were slowing that. Fortunately, she took the hint and walked away.

More posters went up around the surrounding areas that continued to expand as Tricki remained missing. Most people he talked to were helpful. No, they hadn't seen a Pekingese roaming the neighborhood, but they would be on the lookout and let him know if they saw anything. Unfortunately, every party has a pooper. A resident, probably the condo busybody with nothing better to do, berated Roger for posting the sign on a pole in front of the building. She growled that it made the place look trashy and lowered property values. As patiently as he could, (He surprised even himself), he pointed out the pole was on the road right of way, not on condo property, and he was doing nothing wrong. She huffed off telling him he hadn't heard the last of this. He laughed to himself as she left. He was just happy she'd gone away. Some people make things better merely by leaving. *Wonder if she'll take it down when I'm out of sight?*

He posted several signs along US 1 and worked his way west along commercial Barton Boulevard. A few people asked what he was doing, and he explained to them about the missing dog. Yes, they had seen a Pekingese. Roger thanked them for their help but wondered if it was Tricki they'd seen or the one found dead in the road. More signs went up. At a UPS office and warehouse several blocks off Barton, he talked with several drivers. Two said they'd seen a dog matching Tricki's description. One said it was in the neighborhood, and the other couldn't remember where along his delivery route he'd seen the dog. The drivers all took a poster and said they would be on the lookout, and Roger reminded them of the reward and thanked them.

He grew hungry as the hands on the clock reached the worship position, straight up toward the sky. It was hot that day, so he opted for lunch in the AC at a Wendy's Restaurant. The number one choice sounded good, a big burger, fries, and a cold drink. He selected an ice tea. It came southern style, very sweet, too sweet for his taste. Next time, he'd know better.

At a payphone outside, he dropped a quarter in the slot and called his home number. To his surprise, Lester answered, "Hello."

"Lester, surprised to hear from you. How's the work goin'? Where's Carlos?"

"Work's going fine, Roger. I found a small air conditioner unit that fits right in one of your windows in the front, but Carlos ain't doing so good. Looks like he got sick, threw up, and now sleeping in the trailer. I think he found something for lunch, it didn't agree with him, he puked, and is now sleeping."

"That's not good. I think I better come home."

Lester said, "Yeah, I think you better. I think he got into your beer."

"What? Got into my beer?"

"There's a couple of empty bottles on the kitchen table. He puked on the porch, but K9 cleaned up most of the vomit. The area still smells like stale beer and other things."

Roger planted his palm to his forehead and sighed deeply. "I'll be there shortly. How's K9?"

"It appears she's been up and got her appetite back. Right now, she's sleeping soundly and if I read the expression on her face right, contented and in no pain."

Roger shook his head. A drunk kid and a drunk dog. How was he ever going to explain this? "I'm at the Wendy's on Barton Boulevard in Rockledge. Give me twenty minutes, and I'll be there."

"Sure thing. I'll keep an eye on them till you get here. I got the window out and was about to put the air conditioner in when you called. Be a good time to take a break."

"You're welcome to whatever you can find for lunch."

Lester asked, "Does that include the beer?"

Roger cringed. "Yeah, you're an adult, but don't end up like the others here."

"Not a problem. One beer only for me. I still got to get the thing in and closed up weather tight. Cloudin' up and looks like we could have some rain."

"Only a few clouds here."

Lester said, "Yeah, welcome to Florida. Raining buckets on one side of the street and nothing on the other."

"Yeah, this state has some weird weather. Bye, Lester. I'll see you shortly."

"Sure thing."

Roger got in his truck and headed home. How was he going to explain this to Gloria or anyone else who found out about the incident? Some parent he was. First extended time together with his son, and he gets drunk. What was he going to do? All options seemed bad. Telling the truth seemed the least bad. The excuses he'd come up with didn't ring true at all. The truth it was then. He'd worried about the consequences later.

Oh, Lord, help me.

Chapter 19

Roger had a devil of a time getting his truck through the gate. Donkey was in one of his wanderlust moods and tried to escape, but Roger was faster. There would be no eloping today. Roger had enough problems already.

He parked his truck and could hear the sound of activity on the backside of the trailer. He found Lester putting the finishing touches on the air conditioner installation.

"Looks good. How are things here?" Roger asked.

"It's been interesting. Nothing but interruptions. Bill stopped in for a break from duty and wanted a refreshment and Mrs. Porcher called twice. Carlos' mom called, wanting to know how he was doing, and somewhere in there when not being your phone answering service, I found time to get this thing in. That's how my day has gone."

Could it get any worse? Roger said, "Thanks for takin' the calls. So, our town flatfoot was here for a brew. Did he see Carlos?"

"He did. He knows and wants to have a chat with you."

"I thought as much. Mrs. Porcher wanted to know about her dog, right?"

Lester nodded.

"What did you tell the boy's mom?" Roger said.

"She wanted to talk with him, but I told her he was sleeping. Of course, she wanted to know who I was and where you were."

Roger shook his head and sighed? "Can it get any worse?"

"I hope not, but the circuits and wiring in this old trailer are ancient, and I don't know if it will take the electrical demand the AC unit requires. You may need to upgrade some stuff if it starts blowing fuses. You have a few extra. And don't go putting bigger fuses in if they pop. That will make a real fire hazard, and you don't need that in this old tin can."

"Gotcha. I better check on Carlos and start putting out fires before it gets worse."

"Okay."

Lester went back to work after his most recent interruption. Roger found K9 lying on her mat. The wounds looked about the same, maybe a little better. She slept peacefully. Second-hand beer and painkillers can do that. After that, he walked into the trailer and saw the two empty beer bottles on the kitchen table. A clean spot on his needing attention floor had to be where Carlos threw up. He sat down on the lower bunk bed across the narrow hallway from where the boy snored.

"Carlos, wake up. It's your dad."

He groaned and rolled over.

"Carlos, I need to talk to you."

One bleary eye opened. "What?"

"How do you feel?"

"My head hurts, and the room's spinning."

"I need you to set up." Roger helped him into a sitting position, but he nearly fell over. Roger had to steady him. "What did you have for lunch?"

"SpaghettiOs and soda pop, but it tasted funny."

"That wasn't soda pop. It was my beer. That's not for kids, adults only."

"I thought it was ginger ale. It looked like it, but was a little sour. Is that why I don't feel so good?"

"Yeah, it is. You must promise me you'll never get into my beer again, okay?"

"Sure, Dad. Now, can I go back to sleep? My head still hurts."

Roger said, "I bet it does. Go ahead."

Carlos flopped over and went back to snoring.

Roger shook his head. *One fire suppressed. A bunch more to go.* He heard the phone ring and answered it. "Hello."

"Roger, I hadn't heard from you since this morning. Anything new on my Tricki Woo? Please tell me you found him."

"No, I don't have much more, nothin' good, nothin'. He's still missin'. I got the posters up around your house. I'm workin' my way out from your house in three directions. I searched down by the river but didn't see any signs he'd been there. I meant to stop before I left down there, but I was called away. Had a little family emergency of my own. I hope you understand."

"I do, but will it interfere with your job finding Tricki?"

Roger said, "I see your concern, but I should be able to juggle two balls at once."

"Good. I miss my Tricki so much." She stopped. "I better let you go, so you can find him and take care of your problem."

"Thank you for your concern. I know you're concerned about Tricki. Could you limit your calls? Answering them cuts down on my time and ability to search."

Roger knew his advice likely fell on deaf ears, but he needed to make a point.

"Very well. I shall let you go. Please, oh please, call immediately when you have news, good or bad. Good day, young man."

He heard a click and then a dial tone. He placed the handset down on the phone, and it immediately began ringing. "Now, who can that be? This place is as busy as Grand Central Station. Hello?"

"Roger, Doctor Solomon here. I thought of a few things that may help your search. How's K9?"

"She seems to be okay. She's sleeping peacefully right now. What important info do you have?"

"That's good. The pain killer I gave her was pretty strong. Animals often sleep after the injection. I have two things I want to inform you of in your search. If you were looking for a cat, I'd not go far from the point the animal disappeared. Cats will hole up and hide. Not so with dogs. They may stay around, but when frightened, they run and can run for miles. Let's hope Tricki Woo didn't. And dogs on the hunt will also travel for miles, whether it's seeking prey or female companionship. Tricki would be more of a wanderer looking for fun, from what I know of him."

Roger said, "I had that feelin', too. What was the other thing you wanted to tell me?"

"Watch out for scammers. Someone could see your posters, claim they saw the dog, and want money in exchange for the knowledge they claim to have. Also, you may get a call from a person who says they were visiting the area, saw a lost dog, picked him up, and have now left the area. They'll either ship the dog back or bring him back if you give them money to do so. Do that, and you'll never see the dog or your money again. That's it. Got critters that need attention. Good to hear K9 is okay. Bring her in if anything changes. Got to go. Bye."

"Thanks, Doc. Have a good day. Bye."

He put the handset down on the base. *So far, so good.* But he had this feeling things were going to get worse. He didn't have to wait long for…

Chapter 20

"Roger, it's time to see if we can get you AC," Lester said.

"So, what's left?"

"We plug it in and turn it on. And hope and pray the old electric wiring in this fire trap can hold up."

"So, what could go wrong?"

Lester said, "Several bad things. You got a fire extinguisher handy?"

"I do. Let me get it for you." Roger opened a tiny closet and produced a small fire extinguisher. He handed it to Lester, who examined it closely.

"Well, it's charged and will work on electrical fires. Not all fire extinguishers are created equal. Some have specific purposes. This one's a general purpose one. I'm glad you have one. Never know when you will need it. Do you have a smoke detector in the trailer?"

"No."

"Get one. You never know when something bad will happen, especially when you're sleeping. It could save your life."

Roger said, "I'll pick one up today."

"Good. Now let's see if all is well. Shouldn't take long to see if it can handle the load." Lester plugged the AC unit cord into a wall outlet and turned it on. It buzzed to life and after a blast of hot air, then cool air came out of the vent.

"Looks like it's workin'," Roger said.

"Wait. The next minute or so is critical. Got to see if it can carry the load."

They waited, and cool air continued to flow from the unit. A buzz came from the unit and then the wall receptacle flashed, followed by a puff of smoke. Lester sprayed a puffy white cloud from the fire extinguisher on it. Roger said, "I know that's not good."

"No, it's not. I'm gonna have to run a new circuit to the AC, one that can handle the load."

"So, what's that mean for now?"

"No AC until I run to the hardware store, get additional electrical supplies I need, and install them. Could take the rest of today if I have to jerry-rig it. Quicker if the store has all the right parts. "

Roger said, "Do it. I'll be here with Carlos. Looks like he slept right through the excitement."

"That's why you need a smoke detector. You would sleep right through something going wrong and wake up dead."

"Why don't you pick up one while at the hardware store? I know you'll install it right."

Lester said, "I'll do that. I'll check the electric box and make sure the circuit that blew is off. Safety first."

"Gotcha."

Lester exited the trailer and checked the box. "Yeah, it's off. I'll get going and be back ASAP."

"Sounds good." Roger heard a noise at the road. "Looks like Canaveral Flats' one-man police force is approaching."

"It does. Gotta go. Bye."

Roger watched as the men coordinated getting their vehicles in and out through the gate without Donkey running off. Lester's truck disappeared down Canaveral Flats Boulevard, going east toward US 1. Chief of Police Bill Kenney pulled up to the trailer and got out. He said, "Well, father of the year. Guess you know why I'm here."

"Let me guess. It's about beer. You want one. "

"Yeah, I do want one, but that can wait. It's Carlos and beer I'm concerned about. You could be in some serious trouble, contributing to the delinquency of a minor. You know, that kind of stuff."

"Guess I could be."

"You shouldn't have left him here alone."

Roger sighed, "Nope, no parent of the year award for me. I never raised a youngin' his size before, and I have work to do."

"I heard it all before."

"I'm more worried about what I'm gonna tell his mom. With that Latin temper, she'll go through the roof."

"Likely so."

There was silence between them for a moment.

Roger said, "So what we gonna do?"

"Tell you to be a better parent. Be aware of what's going on. You think you're the first father whose kids have gotten into his adult beverages?"

"Guess not."

"Unfortunately, you won't be the last. I've seen some really bad things happen to teenagers who couldn't handle it. A few even died."

"That's sad. I'll do better."

Bill said, "I know you will. I know what you can do when you put your mind to it."

"I feel like a failure."

"Let me tell you a story. You know, there used to be a house across the street, old man Flanagan's place."

"I vaguely remember it. Not very big and more of a shack than a house."

"That's the place. Old Flanagan got hurt on the job and was never able to collect much Workmen's Comp. He kept hogs to hide the smell of his still, but everybody knew about it. His was some of the best moonshine in the state of Florida."

Roger said, "And your old man, the cop, knew about it?"

"Like I said, he made excellent stuff, and I have more to say that may make you feel better. Old Flanagan went away one weekend and had me and Lester's son lined up to feed his hogs while he was gone. We did that and got into his shine, along with a couple of other boys. We were so drunk, loud, and obnoxious. Naturally, there was hell to pay for everyone. Flanagan was much more careful after that, but it wasn't long afterward that his place caught fire and burned to the ground. Don't think it had anything to with our drunken escapades. He was fortunate to get out but never had any insurance on the place. He went to live with his daughter afterward."

"Guess I'm not the only one that ever had troubles with a boy and alcohol."

"Nor the last."

They said nothing for a few moments.

Bill said. "Flanagan's property's for sale."

"How do you know?"

"It's my business to know. He died recently, and I know his daughter wants to sell it quickly. It's buildable, unlike many of the lots in Canaveral Flats. You got electric lines, a water connection, and even a septic tank. Flanagan was one of the first to have indoor plumbing, even if his place was a shack. You should consider it."

"Reasonable you say?"

"She's motivated. Oh, and one more thing, the property on your west side is also for sale."

"It's kind of low and swampy," Roger said.

"The front's not, and it would make more range for your donkey."

"He's not my donkey, He's just…He's just a guest here. Though you were lookin' for a home for him, right?"

"You know how that's gone."

"Yeah. You quit lookin', and he's still here."

"Keeps your grass cut, and protects your place. Fertilizes it, too."

Roger said, "I can't argue with that, but it sure would be nicer for him if he had a proper home with kids and such."

Bill gazed at the donkey as he grazed. "Looks like he's content and doing fine now. Lot better than being put down like was suggested."

"Guess so. What do they want for the second property?"

"Not sure, but I think it would be reasonable. Look into it. Happening Realty has it listed."

"Thanks, I may just do that."

Roger's phone rang. He looked at the caller ID. Mrs. Porcher. "I better take this call. It's the lady I'm workin' for tryin' to find her lost Pekingese." He pickup up the phone. "Hello, Mrs. Porcher. Why are you calling back so soon? What? A man called and says he has Tricki Woo. He saw the posters and knew he found my Tricki Woo. He'll bring him right over and wants the reward. How much are you giving him? One thousand dollars?"

Bill asked, "Is she alone?"

"Are you alone? Yes. Why do I ask?"

Bill said, "I need to speak with her." He took the phone. "Mrs. Porcher, this is Bill Kenney, Chief of Police in Canaveral Flats. Listen carefully. What you're saying has thrown up all kinds of red flags for my cop senses. This man could be a crook, a criminal looking to do you harm. He could take your money and harm you.

Call the Rockledge Police and have them come immediately. Do not open your door to this man. It may be nothing, but it could be trouble. We don't want to take the chance. I know he sounded nice. That's how criminals work. You will. Good. Again, do not open the door and let him in. Thank you, Mrs. Porcher. You want to speak to Roger? Make it quick and call the police." He handed the phone to Roger.

"Hello. Yes, Mrs. Porcher. You want him back. So do I, but hang up and do what my friend, the Chief of Police, has told you. You could be in danger. Don't want to take chances. Yes. Goodbye, Mrs. Porcher."

Roger hung up the phone. "A scam?"

"Sure does sound like it. A vulnerable old lady with money and thinking only about how bad she misses her pet. Let me use your phone. I know a direct line number for the local police down there."

"Sure."

Bill was soon talking to his contacts in the Rockledge Police Department. They said they would send someone right over. While he did that, Roger called Officer Nyquist on his cell phone. He was on duty. Roger explained the situation, and he said he would drive right over and check on Mrs. Porcher.

Roger said, "Is there anythin' we can do?"

"Don't think so. Now we wait and hope for the best."

"That's the hard part."

"Yeah. Cross your fingers. We've done what we can from here. Now it's up to Mrs. Porcher and the Rockledge Police."

Roger said, "I got a bad feelin' about this."

"Yeah, me, too."

Chapter 21

Roger no more than had put the phone down when it rang again. "Hello. Why Gloria, so good to hear from you. How's the conference goin'? That's good. Glad you're enjoyin' your time in Georgia. Me? Workin' a case. Which one? Believe it or not, it's not with law enforcement. What is it? I'm lookin' for a lost dog. Hey, quit your laughin'. This little lost dog's very important to an old lady, and she's more than willin' to pay handsomely to have him back.

"Carlos? He's not available right now. He's sleepin', takin' a nap. Wasn't feelin' so hot. You know how rest will revive you. No. I don't think it's anythin' serious. Yes, I'll take him to the doctor if he needs it. He's in good hands with me. You can depend on me. Thanks, Gloria. You have a super time there and don't worry about Carlos. I'll call immediately if there's anything you need to know. Thanks, Gloria. Bye."

Roger put the receiver down on the base and sighed.

Bill said, "Looks like you dodged the bullet for now. You know the full truth will come out, and she's not going to be happy."

"I know. Now I have to figure a cover story with enough truth in it to keep her from wantin' to kill me."

"She may want to kill you no matter how well you spin this."

"True, but I bought myself some time. You know how puttin' a little time and space between the incident and her findin' out could cool her down."

Bill said, "Maybe, but you know how women can be."

"Yeah. I'm sure I'm gonna have to face the wrath of Gloria. Can't be any worse than a Klingon, can it?"

"Probably not, but Klingons aren't real. Gloria is."

Roger said, "Any suggestions?"

"No. I'm sure you'll come up with something."

"Not gettin' involved at all?"

"Not on your life," Bill said. "It's your mess. You're going to have to deal with it."

"Chicken."

"You betcha. A live chicken is better than a dead duck any day."

"Good point," Roger said. "Life sure can be interestin' with its daily challenges."

"Very true."

"How are you and my cousin Suzie gettin' along? She still rentin' your efficiency at your place? You are behavin' yourself and not takin' advantage of the situation?"

"I am being a perfect gentleman with her, not that it's any of your business. She's working a lot, and I hardly see her. I did take her out to lunch at Kelsey's one day we both had off work. We had a good time. Took a walk down by the river at Nichol Park. Saw a couple of dolphins feeding on mullet. The latter were hopping out of the water trying to get away and not be eaten."

Roger said, "That will kind of motivate you."

"My old place had another plumbing leak, and she fixed it. She's pretty good at it. Makes a dandy powder puff plumber. I heard you had some problems. Bet she'd help if you ever need a plumber."

Roger cringed and snarled. "Lester told you about my plumbin' issues, didn't he?"

"I'll never tell. Be glad you have people willing to help you when you get in a jam."

"Guess you're right. Wonder how things are goin' at Mrs. Porcher's?"

"I've been wondering about that, too. I wish we could have run right down there, but it's too far. Expect we'll hear something soon," Bill said.

At that time, the phone rang, and Roger grabbed it. Hello? Lester, what's up?" Roger listened for a few moments and said, "Lester, my skills are in forensics, not home repair. You get what you think is best, okay? Fine, Lester. Goodbye."

Roger said, "Lester wanted to know what parts I wanted, somethin' about poles."

"Can't say I'm much of an electrician either. Lester won't do you wrong."

"I know that. That's why I told him to get what he thought was best."

The phone rang again, and Roger grabbed it. "Hello? Who is this? Roger Pyles. You want to speak to Bill Kenney? Yeah, he's right here." Roger handed the phone to Bill.

"Hello? Bill Kenney here. Officer Nyquist. How are things? Uh-huh." Pause. "Uh-huh." Another pause. "Un-huh. Glad it all worked out. Thanks for calling and letting us know. 10-4."

"What happened?"

"The guy came and tried to break into Mrs. Porcher's house. The cops arrived just as he was going through her door. He broke the door window glass to get in."

"Did she get hurt?"

"No. She had a gun on him and was asking him if he was ready to meet Jesus because if he didn't stand still and took a step toward her, he would very soon. He was more than willing to surrender to us, so he could get away from the crazy old lady with the **big** gun."

Roger laughed. "He's lucky she didn't shoot him."

"In this state, you can if they're inside your house, and nothing will happen. Some of those thieves never thieved again. No trial necessary."

"Did he say what kind of gun she had?"

"A small Walther 9mm handgun that fits her hand and doesn't have a lot of recoil. Good gun. I have a 40 caliber Walther I like. It's got a little more kick and stopping power. You ought to come to the range and try it out."

"Okay, sometime in the near future," Roger said.

"Ooohh." A moan came from the trailer, and Carlos appeared at the door. He was wobbly-legged, and his hair was in disarray. "I don't feel so good."

Roger said, "I was wonderin' how long you were goin' to sleep."

Carlos groaned and sat down on the couch.

Bill said, "Guess I better leave. Places to go. Bad guys to catch. Glad it all worked out with Mrs. Porcher."

"Till next time, Bill. I'll see what I can do for Carlos."

"Sure thing."

Roger went into the trailer and Bill left. He headed to his truck and soon was gone.

"Well, son. Are you hungry?"

"A little, but not much. My head hurts and my tummy's queasy."

"You know why?"

"You got into my beer."

"Oh. It looked like ginger ale, but it was kinda sour."

Roger said, "You drank two."

"About one and a half. I spilled the rest when I got sick, then I laid down and fell asleep."

"Carlos, you have to stay out of my beer. Alcohol isn't good for kids. A lot of adults have trouble with it, too. Promise you won't do it again."

"I promise. Now, can I go back to sleep?"

"Okay, Daddy still loves you, even when you do wrong."

Carlos tried to smile, and he shook his head a little. He hugged Roger, who held him tight. Then he began to cry. "Mom isn't going to like this."

"It's okay. I'll deal with your mom. I'll take the punishment, not you. Get some more rest and you'll feel better."

"Okay." He lay on the bed and was soon sound asleep.

What a day this has been. Glad K9 seems to be doin' better. Lester'll take care of the AC and electrical. Guess the father of the year ain't goin' to jail for child abuse. And glad Mrs. Porcher is okay, no harm done to her, but what am I goin' to tell Gloria. Brain don't fail me now.

He heard a vehicle coming down the driveway. Lester. They should have AC tonight. What else could go wrong?

His thoughts were interrupted by a ringing phone.

Chapter 22

"Hello."

"Mr. Pyles, my name's Charley Smith. I'm a salesman for Space Coast Memorial Gardens. I was wondering if you've made any plans for when you leave this world. Decisions such as this shouldn't be left to your grieving family when our time comes. It's better to take care of them ahead of time."

"You're tryin' to sell me a burial plot?"

"I can, but our company can provide you with everything you need. We have an all-inclusive funeral package. Don't leave this burden on your family."

Roger laughed. "Well, I appreciate you telling me upfront what you're sellin' and bein' real friendly about it. Honesty is the best policy. I've had others try to sell me a plot and were kind of pushy about it. I usually tell them my wife and me have an agreement. Whichever one goes first, the other will wait until we get stiff, and then they're to take a croquet mallet and drive us in the ground until we disappear."

Charley laughed. "That's a good one. A new one on me. I thought I'd heard them all. For a minute, I thought you were going to tell me to just leave your body among the rocks or let the vultures eat your body laid on a high platform."

"Guess there're some unique ways of gettin' rid of bodies. A funeral pyre."

"You forgot Soylent Green."

Roger chuckled. "Yeah, that movie had a surprise endin', for sure. I don't think I'm in the market for what you're sellin' today. You wouldn't happen to have seen a Pekingese out on walkabout, have you?

"Tricki Woo?"

"How did you know?"

"I saw the posters. I'm a neighbor of Mrs. Porcher and I thought that was him on the be on the lookout paper. He gets out of her fenced-in yard regularly, comes and visits my dogs, and goes home when he gets hot and tired. Everyone in the neighborhood knows Tricki Woo."

Roger said, "Have you seen him?"

"Come to think about it, I did see a dead dog that looked like him on Barton Boulevard."

"Yeah, I know about that one. It looked a lot like him, but wasn't. Couldn't find the owner, and buried him on the sand hill to the west of Mrs. Porcher's home."

"Guess that's good and bad. Good it wasn't her dog, but bad for someone else."

Roger said, "Yeah. The search for Tricki will continue."

Charley said, "If I see him, I'll give you a call."

"Thank you."

"Got to go. People are just dying to hear from me. A little graveyard humor."

Roger laughed. "You have a nice day. Bye."

"Bye."

Roger hung up the phone and walked over to where K9 lay. He got down on his hands and knees. "How you doin', girl? Feelin' any better?"

She opened her eyes and wagged her tail a little.

He gently stroked her head. "That's good. You're lookin' some better. Ole Doc got you shot full of antibiotics and vitamins. He said I should bring you back if you're doin' poorly. I may take you in for a checkup, just the same."

She wagged her tail and closed her eyes, but quickly opened them and looked toward the road. Lester was coming. He let himself through the gate, drove down to the trailer, and got out with a bag in his hand.

"Get everythin' you need?" Roger said.

"Think so, but you never know."

"Can I help?"

"Roger, is your electrical skills any better than your plumbing abilities?"

"Don't think so."

"Well, if you want it done tonight, I better do it myself."

Roger frowned. "Alright, but after you're done, I want you to explain what you did."

"Fair enough. How's K9 doing?" Lester said.

"Doin' as well as can be expected. The dead coyote disappeared. Did you bury it?"

"I did. Donkey tried to stomp him flat and nearly succeeded. Sometimes farmers keep donkeys around to drive off predators trying to get their animals."

Roger said, "Yeah, sure am glad he was here or K9 might not be. How long you goin' to be?"

"At least an hour. Probably more."

"Then we need somethin' to eat. Pizza?"

Lester nodded. "Sounds good to me."

"Kelsey's?"

Lester looked at his watch. "They don't deliver yet. Not until next hour."

"I'll get it if you keep an eye on my son. He could be up at any time."

"Sure. Call in the pizza and go get it."

He did, left, and was back in about a half-hour. Lester stopped his work and when they sat down at the table in the kitchen, Carlos awoke. Roger said, "How you feelin'?"

"Better. Do I smell pizza?"

"Come get some. I was beginnin' to think you were gonna sleep more than Rip Van Winkle?"

"Who?"

"Never mind. Come get your pizza."

With three guys eating on it, the pizza didn't have a chance and soon disappeared.

Carlos said, "Think that's the best pizza I ever had."

Lester said, "They got some good food over there. You can't go wrong."

"Are you gonna have the electrical work done tonight?" Roger asked.

"It's almost done. Went quicker than I thought it would. I need to run some more wire and then connect it all. Everything should be much better than before."

An hour later, Roger and Carlos sat in an air-conditioned trailer. Roger paid Lester for his electrical work, which included installing a smoke detector. After a long talk with his son about the dangers of alcohol, they got ready for bed. Roger brought K9 inside for the night, where he could keep an eye on her. He noted Donkey doing sentry duty outside.

After getting Carlos down for the night, Roger laid down on the bed across from him. It had been quite a day. He hoped tomorrow would be better. First off, he'd check all the animal shelters in the area for Tricki Woo. Maybe he'd get lucky. He could use a little luck. Maybe not. Maybe he'd look up Mrs. Porcher's daughter and see if she knew anything about the dog's disappearance. Tricki Woo, where are you?

Chapter 23

Roger woke early. After relieving himself, he checked on K9. She roused a little when he spoke to her and clumsily got to her feet. "Atta girl. I don't think you'll want to run a marathon, but it looks like you're doin' better. Your food's outside. You want some?"

She knew what those words meant and wagged her tail with a little enthusiasm.

"That's good. You have an appetite. Let's see if you can make it down the steps." He opened the door, and the morning warmth hit him. "Looks like it's gonna be a hot one, K9. Let's go."

He held the door open, and she gingerly went down the stairs. "You made it. Good girl." He followed her out and opened the big metal garbage can that held her food. The bag was almost empty, but he found about a half scoop for her. He looked around the porch, but she was not there. Instead, she was outside emptying her bladder. She got up, saw Donkey, and started walking toward him. They stopped two feet apart. K9 raised her nose and sniffed the air. Donkey lowered his head and their noses touched. He made a cooing sound, and she licked his nose. "Well, I'll be. Looks like Donkey wants to know how she's doin' and she's thankin' him."

"Who are you talking to, Dad?"

"Just talking to myself. How long have you been standing there?"

"Not long. I heard you get up and go outside. I went to the bathroom and then wanted to find out what was going on. And I'm hungry. What's for breakfast?"

"I never did make it to the grocery store. Have you ever been to Waffle House, Carlos?"

"No. Mom takes me to McDonald's sometimes, and we get Egg McMuffins. Is it like that?"

"They have something like that, but a whole lot more. You can get about anythin' you can imagine and more."

Carlos said, "When do we leave?"

"As soon as we get properly dressed. I don't think they'd like it if we walked in wearing only our underwear."

"No. I'd be embarrassed. And Mom wouldn't approve."

Roger said, "No, I think not. Let's get dressed. I want to check on Donkey. Make sure he's okay. Never thought to check on him for wounds. Let's get dressed."

They did. Roger checked on Donkey, and they climbed into Roger's truck. "Dad, will K9 be okay?"

"I think so. She seems to be improvin' and I made sure she had water. She barely touched her food and if the cat shows up, she won't eat much. We need to get some groceries for us today, and that includes dog food for you know who."

"The cat eats the dog food?"

"Yeah. She's a stray who adopted me and's just happy to have somethin' to eat. Guess she'd been on her own for some time. She's a terror for any lizards in the neighborhood, birds, and rodents.

I don't have to worry about her, and Donkey pretty much takes care of himself. It will be alright." He stopped. "Did you sleep good?"

"Uh-huh. I don't feel funny anymore. The air conditioning felt good. Made it easier to sleep."

Roger scratched his chin. "First time I slept in AC since I was down in the Keys. It did feel kinda good, but I'm not used to sleepin' all cramped up. Could take a while to get used to it. You must not be starving with all this yammerin'."

A surprised look came to Carlos' face. Quickly, he realized what his father was getting at. He smiled. "I could eat a horse. Let's go."

"How about a donkey? We have one here."

"Naw. Too tough. Break your teeth."

Roger grinned. His kid had his sense of humor. "Okay, let's go."

The ride to Waffle House by the intersection of I 95 and State Route 520 was uneventful. Roger got the last spot in the parking lot. They walked into the small building. Every table and stool at the counter was occupied. Several bikers sat at the bar. Two men in business suits sat next to them, chatting. Some of the tables were full, while others only had one person or two. Waiters and waitresses scurried around, taking orders and delivering food and drinks.

Carlos said, "Now, what do we do, Dad?"

"Guess we wait until a spot opens up."

"Roger, over here." He looked around. At the far end of the building, he saw a hand waving. Pastor Nassey. And now he was waving them to come over. They walked to the table.

"Pastor Nassey. What are you doing here?" Roger said.

"Same as you. Trying to get some breakfast. I had to be in the neighborhood. One of the church shut-ins I want to visit lives nearby. This place is sure busy. Who's the young fella with you?"

"This is Carlos, my son."

A look of surprise came to the pastor's face, but he buried it quickly. "Need a place to sit down? I could use some company."

"Sure." They sat down and Roger opened a menu. "What's good?"

"Just about everything. I don't get here very often."

Roger said, "Me, neither. Hard to find a Waffle House up north."

A skinny woman missing a front tooth took their orders. She brought back two coffees for the men and a glass of orange juice for Carlos and told them it would be about ten minutes before they got their meals. They were short-staffed. One of the cooks called in sick. They said that was okay.

"So, what brings you to this far neck of the woods?" the pastor asked.

"Same as you, breakfast, and I'm lookin' for a lost dog. A lady contacted me. Her dog went missing, and she begged me to see if I could find him. I have reason to believe he may be headed this way. Also, the local dog pound is close, over on Cox Road, and I'm gonna see if he might have been picked up."

"So the great detective is now using his talents to find a dog?"

Roger said, "It's kind of a personal favor to an old lady in Rockledge. After my last case, I needed something lighter. What sort of trouble could I get into?"

"What kind of dog is it, anyway?"

"A Pekingese. Here, let me show you his picture." Roger pulled a folded poster from his pocket, unfolded it, and laid it before the pastor.

Pastor Nassey said, "He sure is a handsome little guy and looks like a happy guy. Why would he run away?"

"We're not sure he ran away. There's a slim possibility he was stolen, but it's most likely the wanderlust struck him. He wasn't neutered."

"I see. A dog in that state of mind can travel a long way in pursuit of happiness. What makes you think he might be around here?"

Roger said, "My client has a daughter with a small farm nearby, and he ended up there on one of his recent walkabouts. She has a bunch of interesting critters that include some female dogs."

"That would explain a lot."

The waitress came with her arms full of food. She sat it down in front of them, though she had to wait while Roger removed the poster on the table. "Here you go, boys. Enjoy."

"That was quick," the pastor said.

"The other cook came in. It was his day off, but time and a half was an offer he could not refuse. Enjoy your meal."

The hungry fellows went right to work, and their meals disappeared quickly. Afterward. They made small talk, and the waitress brought their bill. "Here you go, boys. That was a cute dog you had a picture of. Is it yours?"

Roger spoke, "No, he's lost somewhere in the Cocoa/Rockledge area. I'm tryin' to get him returned to his owner. Have you seen him? There's a reward."

"Well, I was just out at the dumpster getting rid of some trash, and I saw a dog that looks like that eating something laying on the ground that some animal had drug out. We've had trouble with wildlife doing that recently."

"Really?" Roger grabbed the bill. He pulled out a twenty. "This should cover it. Pastor, I got to go. Carlos, come with me."

"Sure, Dad."

They hurried to the odorous dumpster.

"Do you see him, son?"

"No."

Roger surveyed the greater area around the dumpster, and Carlos went around the back.

"There he is," shouted Carlos.

Roger ran around the back. "Where?"

"You just missed him. He went through there." Carlos pointed to a small opening in the bushes.

"Damn," Roger said.

"Mom says you shouldn't talk like that, but she does sometimes."

Roger saw an opening in the bushes and a path that lead back in the direction the dog ran. He started following it, but it was slow going. He went as fast as he could but the thick growth of Brazilian Peppertree made progress hard. From further in the tangle, an excited voice cried out.

"Dad, I found something. It smells funny."

"What?"

"Bones, I think."

"Stay right there. I'm comin'."

Roger fought his way to where Carlos was. He pointed to his find. Yes, it was bones, and Roger knew from experience they were human, and he knew the smell of decaying flesh too well. "Carlos, don't touch anything. Lookin' for the dog will have to wait. We need to get out of here and report what we found."

"We're going to quit looking for Tricki?"

"For now. I think we just found somethin' bad. Very bad."

Chapter 24

Roger used his new cell phone to report his findings, and soon the area near the Waffle House was swarming with police from several jurisdictions. They determined the remains were in the county, not the city of Cocoa, so the county would do the investigation. Deputies secured the area and put up police tape. The CSI team arrived soon afterward and began collecting evidence. Roger was told to stay out of the way even when he identified himself as a Canaveral Flats law officer. Fortunately for him, Deputy Yates, who knew him, showed up and vouched for him.

"Sorry about that," Deputy Yates said. "We've had some problems with people claiming to be cops lately and taking advantage of that. You need to get yourself some official papers and a badge from Canaveral Flats."

Roger laughed. "The Chief of Police did give me a badge. It looked like it came out of a box of Cracker Jack. Canaveral Flats is kind of low to no budget."

"Yeah, I know, but you need something better to avoid confusion in times like this."

"I agree. I'll see what I can do to rectify the situation."

Deputy Yates said, "Seeing how I know you, the CSI team has asked me to take your statement."

"Don't they usually do that?"

"Yeah, but they had to split the team. Seems another body was found this morning south of here, also along the interstate."

"Okay, let's get started."

Deputy Yates asked, "Why were you back there in the woods?"

Roger laughed, "Would you believe I was lookin' for a lost dog? We thought we might have got lucky and found him."

"Who's we?"

"Me and my son, Carlos. We were havin' breakfast at Waffle House. A waitress saw a poster I made with a picture of the dog on it, and she said one like that was eatin' scraps out by their dumpster. I never did see the dog. Carlos said he took off through a rabbit hole in the bushes. As small as he is, he was able to get through it. It was there he stumbled on the bones and an awful smell. I found a way in. When I saw the bones, I knew we had a problem. We backed off and called for law enforcement."

"Where's your son now?"

Roger said, "Sittin' on a bar stool at the counter in the Waffle House. He said he was still hungry, and they had all-you-can-eat pancakes. I tell you, that kid can chug down some food. You would think he had a hollow leg."

Yates laughed. "My mother used to say that about me. God rest her soul. Anything else you care to add?"

"No, not really, but if you or anyone else here sees a Pekingese, please let me know. I want to get the dog back to his owner."

"I'll pass the word." He paused. "I don't like the looks of this. It feels more like a crime scene than a natural death. The coroner will have the final word in this matter."

"That's true. What makes you believe we have a crime scene?"

Yates said, "This isn't the first body we've found lately near the interstate. They've been turning up from Titusville to Palm Bay. This one looks like another young woman. You're friends with the coroner?'

"Yeah, Will Corbett and me know each other."

"He could give you his take on this and maybe some inside information. He should be here in an hour or so once the CSI people get a handle on this."

"Roger said, "I haven't got that much time to wait. I guess I could stop by later. In the meantime, I need to check on Carlos. He's probably ruinin' any chance the restaurant will make a profit today. Are we done for now?"

"I believe so. You can go. I know where to find you if I need you."

Roger pulled a folded poster from his pocket. "Here's a picture of the dog along with my cell phone number on it. I can be reached anywhere I have coverage."

"Cell phone? Don't tell me the old Neanderthal has joined the twentieth century? Not that your home phone ever works."

"How did you know about my landline problems?"

Yates laughed. "Everyone in law enforcement knows about it. They all joke about it. Some even take side bets on it. Will the call go through or not?"

"What odds are they givin'?"

"Just 50-50."

Roger said, "Better than I'd have thought. Now, if we're done, I really need to go check on my pancake devouring son."

"Yeah, we're done. Good luck with finding the dog. I'll call the cell number if anything develops."

"Thanks," Roger said. "Till next time."

Yates nodded, walked to another man, and spoke to him.

Roger headed into the restaurant building. He sat on an empty stool next to Carlos. "Had enough pancakes yet?"

He patted his stomach. "Can I finish this last one?"

"Sure. I'll get a cup of coffee."

Roger sipped at his beverage as Carlos finished the pancake and asked for another. They finished at the same time. Roger got the bill, left the waitress a nice tip, paid for their food, and they were off to check out the county dog pound, AKA, Central Brevard Animal Shelter. Maybe they'd find Tricki Woo among the throng of yelping canines. Maybe not.

Chapter 25

The drive over to the pound was short, just a mile or two. They parked under a tree in the sandy, unpaved lot. The yelping of dogs told them they were in the right place. Several sturdy cages sat on the long porch that ran the length of the building. A white door with paw prints and the word entrance painted on it beckoned them in.

Roger swung it open, and they walked in. The smell of animals, mainly dogs greeted them.

"Welcome to the Humane Society," a young woman said. "How can we help you? Are you looking for a pet to adopt? One that's been lost? Veterinary services? Would you like to volunteer or give a donation? How can we help?"

Roger said, "Thank you for all that information, but first I want to make sure I'm in the right place. This is the county dog pound, right?"

"Some people refer to this place as that, but we're much more than a place for lost animals. We have all the services I mentioned available."

"Are you with the county?"

"Yes and no. We take in some of the lost animals from the county, but we're not part of the county government services. We're an independent organization that served Brevard County's homeless animals since 1952. Are you looking for a pet to adopt?"

"No, lookin' for a stray dog for a woman. I got a dog a while back from the bunch up in Titusville."

She said, "That would be the SPCA, Society for Prevention of Cruelty to Animals. They're similar to us, but a different organization."

"How many different animal places are there in the area?"

"A lot. Some are like us that deal with dogs, cats, and occasionally other domestic pets, Most are private, but the county has similar services in various places in the county. And then there are those organizations that specialize in breeds of dogs like greyhounds. We have the thoroughbred horse group, the bird groups, the wildlife groups, the turtle rescue people, and even groups that rescue animals you would normally see at the circus."

"I didn't know that."

"If you need to adopt anything from a dog to a meerkat, I can point you in the right direction."

Roger laughed. "I don't need another pet. One dog, a cat, and a donkey who's a guest that never left, that's all I need. No, thanks. If you can help me find a lost dog, I'll be more than happy."

"We have some strays. What does the dog look like?"

Roger pulled a folded poster from his pocket. "Here. This is the fella I'm lookin' for."

She took the poster. "A Pekingese. He's a handsome guy. I'd remember him. No, he's not here. Can I keep the poster? I'll put it on our bulletin board. Maybe he'll end up showing up here, or someone visiting will have information and contact you."

"I appreciate that."

"Dad, can I see the dogs and cats?" Carlos asked.

"Okay, but we're not gettin' a pet. You'll have to talk with your mom if you want a pet."

"Mom says no pets are allowed where we live, but I still want to look."

Roger said, "Where do we start?"

She said, "All animals in cages are adoptable. The cats are in that room." She pointed to a door. "And the dogs are down that hallway. Which would you like first?"

"The dogs," Carlos said. I wanna see the dogs."

"Follow me," she said.

They went down the hallway, turned right, and dogs in kennel areas lined both sides of the walkway. Some yelped heartily and put their paws on the chain link fence that separated them.

"Dad, they all look so friendly."

Most of them are. They'd make someone a good pet."

"Can I get one?"

"Carlos, I've got K9, a cat, and a donkey. I don't need another pet, and I don't think your mom would like it one bit if you showed up with a dog I'd let you get."

The young boys face fell. "Yeah, Mom says no pets. They don't allow pets of any kind where we stay."

"Guess they had some bad experiences in the past with irresponsible pet owners."

The attendant nodded, "Yeah, seems like most of the troubles we see that show up here are because of human failure. People treat their pets as people, but forget their animals with their own nature. Dog behavior is different than the way people interact. Have you ever seen people sniffing each other like dogs do?"

Carlos laughed.

"Of course not. Dogs have an incredible sense of smell and they use their noses to identify and remember each other."

Roger grinned. "Yeah, a dog can get more factual info sniffing another dog than you'll ever get from a newspaper or a politician."

She said, "Very true, but we try not to get political around here. Got to remember taking care of animals is our mission."

"Are there any more shelters like this nearby?" Roger asked.

"You've already mentioned the one in the north end of the county. There're several in the south end in Melbourne and Palm Bay, but a dog would have had to have help getting there. If I were looking for a lost dog like you are, I'd keep looking in the local area. Just be careful. Some spots nearby are known for drug activity and gangs."

"Thanks for the heads up. Son, I think we better get back to our search. Lots of dogs here, but no Tricki Woo. The quest is afoot."

"Huh?" Carlos said.

"It means we need to keep lookin'. Let's go." Roger stopped. "Thank you, young lady for your help. I never did catch your name."

"It's Lola. I'm a fifth generation Floridian and a member of the Mosquito Beaters."

"Well, glad to know you, Miss Lola. I'm Roger. And please, if you learn anything about my missing dog, call me ASAP. My cell number's on the poster you have."

"I certainly will, Mr. Roger, not Mr. Rogers, but I hope you return to our neighborhood."

Roger grinned, "I most certainly will if I hear from you. Wish I could stay longer and talk, but I have a job to do."

"Anytime."

She walked them to the front door, said goodbye, and let them out. She watched Roger as he confidently walked away. Those broad shoulders and narrow hips sent a thrill though her.

A voice behind her startled her. "He's sexy, isn't he? Gets your motor running."

She turned to Brenda, her friend. "Was it that obvious?"

"To another woman, but I doubt he barely noticed if at all. Men aren't near as good at reading people as women."

"Very true."

Brenda said, "What was he here for?"

"Looking for a lost dog." She showed the other woman the poster.

"A Pekingese. I saw a dead one in the road on Barton Boulevard yesterday. Wonder if it's the one he's looking for?"

Lola said, "I don't know." She looked out the window, but Roger's truck was on Cox Road and growing smaller. "I'll have to give him a call on his cell phone."

"Hey, Lola, Brenda. A little help here. I need some help with this big dog."

They rushed to help the third woman with the unruly dog. Other things came up, and Lola forgot all about calling Roger, but it was just as well. He and Carlos were busy combing the area around the recent dog sighting and putting up posters. Tricki Woo, where are you?

Chapter 26

"Dad, I'm hungry."

"Again? I thought you ate enough pancakes to carry you for a week. How can you be hungry?"

"Searching for a lost dog's hard work. Anyway, I'm hungry. Mom says I'll eat her out of house and home."

Roger said, "She could be right. It is gettin' close to noon."

"Can we go back to Waffle House? I want some pancakes. And a burger. I need to fill up my hollow leg again."

"Yeah, it seems you do. Now that you mentioned it, I'm gettin' a little hungry myself. Okay, it's back to Waffle House for us."

Five minutes later, they pulled into the restaurant parking lot. Roger got the last spot. He noted the crime tape that ran from the south side of the building, around the dumpster, to another parking lot of the next-door hotel, and then to the woods. When he entered the place, he saw several uniform police officers sitting on bar stools at the counter. They turned and eyed him, and they went back to eating.

The place was full, but a voice called out. "Roger, over here. He saw a hand beckoning. Pastor Nassey. "I've got room at my table for you."

Roger and Carlos walked to the table. "Why, thank you, Pastor." They sat down. "Why are you still here? I thought you'd be back at the church. Any place but here."

"I thought so, too, but God has a way of putting you where you need to be. The visit took longer than I expected, and I got hungry again. You still looking for the dog?"

"Yeah, the one Carlos saw could have been him, but we're not sure. The investigation has the area I wanted to search cordoned off, so that was out. We went over to the humane society, and they were sympathetic, but didn't have Tricki Woo."

A waitress came over. "What can I get you guys to drink?"

They told her, and she returned quickly with coffee for the men and a coke for Carlos. She took their food orders and left.

Roger jumped.

Pastor said, "What's going on?"

"My pocket's vibratin'."

Carlos rolled his eyes. "Dad, it's your phone. Answer it."

He pulled it from his pocket and clumsily answered it. "Hello? Why, Lola? What a pleasant surprise. Yeah, I'm nearby. Do you have Tricki Woo? No. Uh-huh. South Brevard ASPCA. Where's that? Let me get somethin' to write with." The pastor handed him a pen. "Okay, go. Uh-huh. Uh-huh." Roger said nothing as he intensely listened. "Got it. Thanks, Lola. And it was good to meet you, too."

He hung up and looked at the questioning faces. "Lola over at the Humane Society. She did some checking around for a lost Pekingese. Seems someone just turned one in at the ASPCA in Melbourne. And it was found along I 95 near Rockledge. Could be the dog we're lookin' for. Guess I need to take a trip down there and see. We may have just gotten lucky. I won't know until I get a look at him."

"Pastor, how was your visit with the lady?"

"Interesting, to say the least. Mrs. Miller is still slowly deteriorating. By that, I mean she's going downhill faster than we all are. We all get a little closer to death every day, but she's traveling down that road faster than most."

"What's her problem?"

"She had a stroke years ago. It's affected her right side. She's lost the use of her right arm. It's affected her leg on that side, and she walks with great difficulty. Her speech's been affected. Carrying on a conversation is difficult for her. She understands what's going on, but answering is hard. You can tell she has a lot to say, but can only get it in little delayed spurts, usually just a word or two."

Roger said, "That's got to be frustrating for her."

Pastor Nassey said, "You would think so. It sure would be for me, but she seems to have accepted it, and's been making the best of it. She lets me know she spends a lot of her waking time praying. She says God doesn't have any trouble understanding her. Mrs. Miller's face nearly glowed when she got those twisted words out, and she saw I understood her. You can't do that all the time.

"Must be tough on her. She's a prayer warrior. When God gives out the rewards in Heaven, she'll have plenty. I worry about some people, especially some in politics, who say they're good

137

Catholics, but are working unrelentingly to drive God out of our schools, government, and the public square. They don't trust in God. They trust in government. That's never worked out well anywhere on this planet. They've sowed the wind and are now reaping the whirlwind. Abortion, violence, human abuse and trafficking, porn, drugs, alcohol, corruption, suicide, and families falling apart. The list goes on.

"People are wondering what's going on in our country. Read the newspapers or check the nightly news, and you'll see what happens to a nation that rejects God. Darkness creeps in and tries to take over. What did they expect would happen when you drive God out of society?" He stopped. "Pardon me for getting all worked up and climbing on my soapbox."

"So, what's the answer, Pastor? Is there one or is it just gonna get worse until the world either implodes or explodes or both?"

"There is an answer. I believe God gave us a manual for life, and it's called the Bible. Though many have attacked it, or tried to ban, or suppress it over the millenniums, it's still there, a shining light full of glorious promises, guidance, and hope." He paused. "Roger, I guess you hit a hot button. Sorry for the rant."

"That's okay. You feel better gettin' it out? I know I do when I let it out like that."

The pastor laughed and smiled. "Thank you for your understanding. You know, Roger, if I believed in reincarnation, which I don't, I'd think you were a preacher in a past life."

"Now, that is funny. Me, a preacher. Surprised you didn't say a hyena."

Pastor Nassey laughed, "God can use anyone. If he can use me, I know he can use anyone."

The waitress showed up with their food. "Here you go, boys. Enjoy."

She placed their meals down in front of them and left. Pastor blessed the food with a brief prayer, and they chowed down hungrily. After they finished, they made small talk for a while before the conversation became more serious.

Pastor said. "The coroner left shortly before you arrived. He had what he needed here and needed to get to Melbourne quickly about another pickup."

"I know what you're talkin' about. Where was this one?"

"If you're going to the ASPCA, you'll go right by it. There's a big homeless camp about a quarter-mile off the interstate. One of the people living there flagged down a cop and reported a dead body."

"Thanks for the info, Pastor. I better get goin'. Time's rollin' on like a river. Come on Carlos. Let's go." They got up. "Till next time."

"You too, Roger."

Roger found their waitress who gave him his bill and the pastor's, as well. He smiled to himself as he imagined the look on the pastor's face when he found out his meal had been paid for. He paid the tabs and told her to keep the change. She smiled and wished him a good day.

Traffic was heavy on State Route 520, and it took some time to find an opening. At the first light, he made a U-turn, and two lights later, they took a left on the interstate access road. Traffic was moderate on the four-lane highway going south, but slowing to a crawl northbound.

"Must have been an accident," Roger said.

Carlos nodded but said nothing.

Wonder if the dog could be Tricki Woo? Guess I'll find out soon. And I wonder how the coroner's makin' out. Why have I got a really bad feelin' about this? Why?

Chapter 27

Roger pulled his truck out onto the interstate and merged into traffic. The posted speed limit of 70 mph seemed just a suggestion to most of the travelers.

"Dad, it's hot. Can we roll up the windows and you turn on the AC?"

Roger said, "Today, we can. About a week ago, we couldn't. The truck's AC broke a good while back and I never got around to gettin' it fixed, but a couple of weeks ago, when it was really hot, I decided to have it fixed. Scott, a shade tree mechanic in the Flats, worked me in his schedule and fixed it. I'd been without it for so long; that I forgot to turn it on. Tell me if you get too cold. It got fixed so good, it could freeze a polar bear at the North Pole."

Carlos' eyes widened. "That's cold. Bet there's lots of snow at the North Pole. I never seen snow. What's it like?"

"That depends. Sometimes it's powdery and fluffy. Sometimes it's wet and heavy, but it's always cold. Maybe one of these days I can take you up north in the wintertime, and you can get your fill of snow. I think I like the weather in Florida better, but a change of seasons is nice, too."

"My teacher at school says the earth's getting warmer, and the polar bears will die."

"Son, from what I can see, the climate on this planet's always changing and always has been. Ever heard of Greenland?"

"Uh-huh."

Roger said, "It's a big island way up north in the Arctic where you find polar bears, and it has lots of ice and white snow."

"Why do they call it Greenland then?"

"Because a thousand years ago, when Vikings were crossing the northern Atlantic in their ships, it was green with lots of pasture for farm animals, so they called it Greenland."

"Viking. Those were the guys with horns on their helmets."

"No, hate to burst your bubble, but real Vikings never had horns on their helmets. Son, I think your teacher means well. At least, I hope she does, but not everythin' they tell you in school is true. When I was young, our science class books had Ernst Haeckel's diagrams of human embryos, that's a baby growing inside his mommy, startin' out lookin' like a fish, then an amphibian, then a mammal, and finally a human baby. The book said it reflected our evolutionary progression in nature, but that theory was known to be false when I was in school."

Carlos said, "It's in my science book at school."

Roger said, "Not surprised. People like to hold on to bad ideas and not want to change or admit they were wrong, and scientists and teachers are no different. There's a bunch of stuff in school books that are not completely accurate. Schools reward you for repeatin' what they say, not for learnin' to think. Your teacher isn't an authority on everything. She may only be repeating what she was taught which could be wrong." He stopped. "Son, don't be afraid of questionin' me on what I believe and why. Questions sharpen our mind and help us get to the truth whether it's in science or what we believe about life."

Carlos seemed to be thinking about what his father said. "Dad, do you think Tricki Woo could get way far away quickly?"

"Only if he had help. And the only way I know to be sure if the dog they have is Tricki is to take a look at him. Wish there was some kind of way to easily send pictures, but there isn't. Maybe someday there will be."

"My teacher says there will be."

Roger said, "I believe she's right on that one. I agree with her. If we can go from a horse and buggy to the moon in a lifetime, we should be able to figure out how everyone can share pictures. Someone will figure it out and make lots of money when they do."

Carlos was silent for a few moments. "Dad, I'm sleepy. Can I take a nap while you drive?"

"Sure. I'm not surprised you're sleepy. All the blood in your body must be busy tryin' to digest all that grub you ate."

"Mom says the way I eat, I put her in the poorhouse, whatever that is."

"Wait until you're a teenager. She ain't seen nothin' yet, just like they say in the song."

"Huh?"

Roger said, "Never mind. Before you were born. Get some sleep."

"Okay, Dad."

Carlos kicked back and closed his eyes while Roger drove south on the interstate highway. It was pastureland on both sides, but the area was developing fast and he wondered how soon the cows would disappear, and buildings of all kinds would spring up.

He felt a tingling in his pocket. With some difficulty, he pulled the phone from his pocket and answered. "Hello? Mrs. Porcher. Is everythin' alright? Good. No more surprises at your door. No, I haven't found Tricki, but I've been lookin'. Followin' up on a couple of leads, but nothin' concrete. Yes, I'll be sure to let you know if somethin' happens. SON OF A BITCH! Sorry, Mrs. Porcher. I'm drivin' down I 95 and some…person cut in. He nearly hit me. Thank you, Mrs. Porcher. I know I shouldn't drive and talk on the phone. You take care. Bye."

Roger exhaled and blessed the driver some more under his breath. No point in waking Carlos. *Where's a cop when you need one?* The speeding driver continued to weave in and out of traffic and soon disappeared.

Roger wondered if the dog in Melbourne was the one he sought. He hoped it was Tricki Woo they found, but his luck hadn't been good so far today. And what of the second dead body? Was it connected to the other one found by the Waffle House? Maybe the coroner could give him a minute and tell him some details about what they'd found. Roger wondered how Gloria was doing at the conference in Georgia. Was she behaving herself or taking a walk on the wild side like she had with him in Vegas when they'd slipped up and made Carlos? He was so glad she'd kept him. He was his only child living today and a good reason to live. Would there be any more kids in his future? He doubted it, but you never know. If ten years ago, someone had told him he'd be where he was today, he'd thought they were crazy. Maybe the pastor was right; all things happen for a reason. And sometimes it can take a decade to see that.

144

Going to the Dogs

He saw blue lights up ahead and eased into the passing lane. An unmarked patrol car had pulled over the crazy driver. *Well, looks like one prayer's been answered.* Maybe his luck was changing.

He took the exit off the interstate, turned left at the light, and saw the police cars about a half-mile down the road. None had their lights on. That had to be where the body was. Wonder what else they found?

Chapter 28

Roger pulled his truck to the shoulder along the busy highway, and a Brevard County Deputy approached him. Roger rolled down his window.

"No stopping. You need to get moving," the Deputy said.

"I'm Roger Pyles, Canaveral Flats Police. Is the coroner here? I need to speak with him."

The deputy eyes him suspiciously. "Let's see some identification."

Roger said flatly. "I don't have any."

"Then get moving."

"It's okay, deputy. I know him," a third voice nearby said. "He's who he says he is."

Their heads turned to see who was talking. Will Corbett.

The deputy nodded. "Looks like you got the good guy stamp of approval. Pull your vehicle off the road as far as possible."

"Thanks, deputy." Roger moved his truck and roused the boy. "Carlos, I need to get out and talk with some policemen. I can leave the truck runnin' with the AC on, and you can continue your nap. Keep the doors locked. When I'm done, I'll peck on the window and then you let me in. Do you understand?"

"Sure. Go back to sleep and open up when you get back."

"That's the plan. I shouldn't be too long, I hope."

"Okay, dad."

Roger exited the truck and walked toward the gathering of people. He turned and saw Carlos watching him. His head disappeared from view.

Good. I hope he can get some rest. Roger saw the county coroner, Will Corbitt, and went to him.

"Hello, Roger. What brings you to this neck of the woods? Don't tell me you were just passing through, got curious, and had to stop and see what was going on?"

"I know you talked with Pastor Nassey, and I'm sure he told you I found the other body by the Waffle House."

"He did."

"I saw him after you left to come down here. He said you had to investigate another found body."

"Yeah, a fellow living in the nearby homeless camp smelled something bad, saw a decomposing body, walked to the closest gas station, and reported it to a store clerk. She called for the cops. They came and wanted me to take a look along with the CSI team."

"What can you tell me?"

Will said, "This one's a lot fresher than the last. She hasn't been there very long, a day or so, no more. Decomposition's not so bad yet, but she does stink pretty bad, unlike the one you found."

Roger said, "Yeah, that one was little more than bones. Was it a woman, too?"

"It was. I could tell from the hip bones we recovered. I was lucky to find the hyoid bone, and it was broken."

"Sounds like strangulation to me. What about this one?"

"There're some suspicious markings on her neck, but I won't know for sure until I get her back to the morgue and do a proper examination."

Roger asked, "Do you think these two cases could be related?"

"Very possible, but too early to tell for certain. I've got several Jane Does at the morgue we've found dumped along the interstate. A few were along the highway, but most bodies were near exits. None were over a mile from I 95, but there could be others that haven't been found. They ranged from skeletons to about a week old. This is the freshest one yet. Maybe our killer is running out of good places to dump his victims."

"Sounds to me like we could have a serial killer on the loose."

Will nodded, "If I was a betting man, I'd give you two-to-one odds in favor."

"I believe I'd take those odds."

"So, you're a pet detective now? Isn't that a little out of your usual realm of investigative work?"

Roger said, "Well, an old lady pretty much begged me to find her dog. I felt sorry for her at first. She can be a real pain in the keister at times. I thought she was goin' drive me crazy at first, but

I'm beginnin' to think she's a spunky old dame, and I want to see she's reunited with her Pekingese. The animal shelter in Melbourne said they'd just had one turned in, and he was found along the interstate near Rockledge."

"And it could be the one you're looking for?"

"That's it in a nutshell. I won't know until I see him."

Someone yelled for the coroner.

Will said, "Looks like the CSI team needs me more. I have to go. Good luck, Mr. Pet Detective." He snickered.

"Eat your heart out, Will. Go pick up your cold one."

Will laughed and walked to the crime scene.

Roger returned to the truck and woke Carlos. Soon they were heading east on Eau Gallie Boulevard. Five minutes later, they pulled into the parking lot of the animal shelter. It was a little more modern than the one in West Cocoa but in need of repairs. Roger and Carlos went into the building and introduced themselves. The Pekingese was in the back. A young woman took him there, but it was not Tricki Woo. This dog was mainly white with a black face, and it was female.

"Cute dog," Roger said, "But it's not the one I'm lookin' for. My Pekingese has a lot of brown on him, and yes, the dog I'm searchin' for is a fully equipped male. This is the only one you have, right?"

The young woman said, "This is the only Pekingese we have, but we have lots of animals to adopt."

"No, not today. Just lookin' for a missin' dog named Tricki Woo. I have a poster you can keep. If he does show up, please call me immediately. My phone number's listed on the notice."

She took the poster. "If he shows up, I'll make sure you get a call. We like happy endings where animals are reunited with their owners."

"Thank you. We'll find our way out."

"Good luck with your search."

"Thanks."

They found their way to the exit and left. Roger started his truck and his phone rang. He looked at the number. It wasn't Mrs. Porcher. Who could it be?

Chapter 29

"Hello." Roger listened for a moment. "No. I don't need a cemetery plot at this time, though I may soon." A wicked smile came to his face. "Can I dig the graves myself in the middle of the night with no questions asked? Why? You see, I have this list I'm workin' down, and I'm runnin' out of places to hide the bodies. A cemetery would be the ideal spot. You know, hide them in plain sight." Click. "Hello?" Roger chuckled.

Carlos said, "Who you gonna bury, Dad?"

Roger smiled. "No one. I don't have anyone to bury, but you never know."

"Dad, quit pulling my leg. That's not legal what you're thinking."

Roger's smile grew broader. "You're right. I get these calls all the time from places wantin' me to buy a gravesite, and it's kind of irritatin' after a while. How they got my new number so quickly is beyond me. People callin' you on the phone tryin' to sell you something you don't want or need can bring out the worst in a person. I'm not the only one who hates the calls. One person I know answers sales calls in either one of two ways based on the mood he's in. He lets them start their spiel and then he says, 'There's blood everywhere. I didn't mean to do it.' Or he says, 'This is Detective Smith of the Sheriff's department. The man you want to talk to is lying dead on the floor with a nasty wound in his head. If you knew him, we'd like to speak with you at our downtown office. Could you come right over? Just tell them at the desk why you're there, and they'll direct you where to go.'"

Carlos said, "That's kind of creepy."

"And maybe a little underhanded, but they quickly hang up, go away, and never call back, which is what my friend wanted anyway."

The young boy looked at his father with interest. "I'll tell mom. She gets really mad when they call her."

"That may not be the best thing to do. Moms don't always see the humor in some things, and this is one of those. You get my drift?"

Carlos said, "I think so. It's a guy thing."

"Yes. A special guy thing not to be shared. It a double-top-secret thingy."

"I understand. No sharing."

"That's right. You catch on fast."

Roger's phone began to ring again, but he tried to ignore it.

Carlos said, "Aren't you gonna answer it?"

Roger looked at the number on caller ID. "I think I better. It's Mrs. Porcher." He hit the answer button. "Hello, Mrs. Porcher. Yes, I've been to the animal shelter in Melbourne. It was a Pekingese just as I was told, but no, it wasn't our Tricki Woo. No, wrong color and unless he changed his sex, it wasn't your dog. Yes, she was a nice dog. I'd say about three years old, but I'm no expert on dog age, but she did seem the same age as Tricki. Yes, a very nice dog. A little frightened, but that's to be expected. Yes, Mrs. Porcher, I'll keep lookin' for him. Thank you. Goodbye."

"Old lady who wants her dog back?" Carlos said.

"Yeah, she sure is missin' him. Sometimes I think people miss their pets more than their own family."

An introspective expression came to Carlos' face, but he said nothing.

Roger's phone began to ring once more. He rolled his eyes. "Not again. Who can that be?" He looked at the number. "Guess I'll soon find out. Hello." Pause. "Yes, we are lookin' for a missin' Pekingese. You have him? Good. Where are you? Maine. You were vacationin' in Florida, and you found him runnin' along the highway? Yes, there's a reward. What? You need money to send him back? How much? That's a lot. Uh huh. Uh huh. What's your address? I'll come get him. Yes, I'll come get him. No, it won't be any trouble at all." Click. "Hello? Hello?"

"What happened, Dad?"

"He hung up."

"He hung up?"

"Yeah, it was a scam. He didn't have Tricki Woo, and he wasn't in Maine. You can take that to the bank. I'd send him the money and never hear from him again. No dog and we'd be out the money, and Mrs. Porcher would be very sad. I won't tell her about the call. It would only upset her to think another person's tryin' to take advantage of her situation."

"So watcha gonna do?"

"I got several ideas. When we get back to Cocoa, we have several options."

"I think our best bet is to look around the Waffle Hut area and see if the little Pekingese has been spotted again or if we can find him. Roger said. "Maybe we'll get lucky. I can call the animal shelter north in Titusville and inquire if they may have picked up a dog like Tricki Woo. And I really need to go over to the little farm where Mrs. Porcher's daughter lives. Tricki showed up there on one of his previous adventures. He may do that again. The daughter may know where her brother is and if he could be involved in Tricki's disappearance."

"Okay, Dad. Maybe we can find him. Bet he won't be like that doggy in the window."

"Patti Page sang that old song. How did you know about it? It was old when I was young."

"Mom sings it sometimes. She likes that hound dog song, too."

Roger said, "The one by Elvis."

"I think so. She pretends she's got a mic in her hand and starts swinging her body all over the place, mainly her hips, and belts out about the dog crying all the time."

Roger smiled. "Now that is interestin'. I think I can see her dancin' around bombinatin' all over the place."

Carlos appeared puzzled. "Not sure if she was bombinatin' or not, but it sure can be funny. I tried not to let her see me laugh, but sometimes she catches me and makes me sing along."

Roger grinned. "That would be a sight to behold."

"Sometimes she sings in the shower. I think she sounds better in there."

Roger said, "Most people do," and then he laughed.

"I'm not sure she'd like it if she knew I told you."

"I understand. I wouldn't say you told me."

"Thanks, Dad."

They drove along in silence looking at the swampland and cows in the pasture.

Roger said, "Take it all in, son. Don't know how long it's gonna stay like this. The company that owns this area wants to turn this into a new town called Viera. Pretty soon there could be houses coming up like mushrooms after a rainstorm, and no more cows."

"Think I like the cows."

"Lots of people think the same way. Seems like people want to shut the door to development once they move in. The old-timers like to talk about how the county only had 25,000 people before the Space Center came. Guess we have ten times that number now, and it's still growin'".

Carlos said, "That's a lot of people."

"The state's growin' rapidly. Some folks say Florida will pass New York up in population in the near future. It's hard to stop progress."

They passed the Fiske Boulevard exit to Rockledge and in about four minutes, exited east onto State Route 520. The Waffle House was on the right. Roger pulled into the parking lot and found a spot near the yellow crime tape. "Wait here a minute. I'll see if I can learn anything more about the dog and the bones we found."

"Okay, Dad."

Roger got out and a deputy stopped him at the tape. Carlos watched, and he could tell the conversation was tense. Roger soon returned to the truck and got in.

'What's wrong?"

"He won't tell me anything about the bones even though I told him we discovered them. He wanted to see some ID when I told him I didn't have any, but I thought everyone in the county had heard of Roger Pyles and his investigatin' skills. Just my luck to find one that didn't. I got to get me a badge from Canaveral Flats PD when I run into idiots like him." Roger seethed. "Guess I shouldn't get so mad. He was right about stoppin' me. He did tell me no one had seen a Pekingese wanderin' around. Either Tricki has bedded down and is hidin', which I doubt, or he's taken off. My bet's on the latter."

Carlos said, "So what do we do?"

"We drive around and see what we can find. If we don't run across Tricki, we head to the daughter's place. Sound good?"

"Sounds good."

They drove through several neighborhoods. No Tricki Woo, but Roger noticed people eye him with suspicion. He drove on to a group of row houses. A young man was standing on the corner. Roger stopped and rolled down his window. "Hey, Buddy. I'm lookin' for somethin'."

"Like what?"

"A little brown Pekingese."

"The man looked puzzled. "Pekingese? What's that? All I got are rocks."

"Rocks? What makes you think I want a rock?"

"Everyone comes here for rocks. I got some good stuff."

"You mean some drugs?"

"Whatever."

"I'm lookin' for a lost dog, a Pekingese. Seen one lately?"

"No. You ain't looking for rocks to get high? What are you, some kind of cop?"

Roger didn't like the way the conversation was going. "I'm lookin' for a little lost dog, nothing more."

"I ain't seen your dog."

"Thanks," Roger said. "I'll get goin'. Have a nice day."

The man grunted, and Roger drove off.

"What was that about, Dad?"

"Guy wanted to sell me some drugs. Bad stuff." He glanced in the rearview mirror and saw the man eyeing Roger's truck. A car pulled up to the man, and he exchanged a small packet for some money. "Yeah, Carlos. We just had an encounter with a drug peddler. Let's see if we can find our lost dog. I can report this later."

"Okay, Dad."

Roger headed toward Mrs. Porcher's daughter's small farm. Maybe Tricki was there. He thought of the drug dealer. Some people think of Florida as a kind of Eden, but even Paradise had a snake, and this place was no different.

Chapter 30

Roger took a left at the intersection onto Pluckebaum Road. The road was no longer paved and Roger's truck bounced along on the sand washboard surface.

"Slow down, Dad. I nearly got bounced off the seat. You're killing my butt."

Roger let his foot off the gas petal, and the truck slowed. "Sorry about that. I was thinkin' what I would say to Bridget, Mrs. Porcher's daughter. They don't get along, I've been told, and I'm not sure if we'll be welcomed pleasantly or not. Guess we'll soon find out. We should be there in another half-mile."

They passed a big sign by the road that said, Jesus Road Service.

Roger said, "Looks like Jesus must be branchin' out. Not only is He in the rescuin' broken down souls on the highway of life, He's towin' vehicles in, too."

Carlos rolled his eyes and shook his head. "Dad, I think the guy is Spanish, and it's pronounced, hey-zyhs."

Roger turned his head and smirked. "Yeah, I think you're right. I was just tryin' to have some fun with you."

"Mom says you're a smart ass, though she told me not to say so."

"Does she?" His eyebrows rose. "Does she also tell you not to say smart ass?"

Carlos said, "Yeah, but she says it and worse when she's mad."

"Yeah, it can be hard not to when you're mad, and English has a lot of good cuss words."

"Huh?"

Roger said, "When I was out in the American Southwest, I hired some Navajo Indians to fence off an archaeological area. I warned them the place was full of rattlesnakes, and they needed to be careful. The lead man told me not to worry. The Navajo people and rattlesnakes were brothers. I said okay and had to leave for a while. When I came back, there were dead snakes everywhere, and he was swearin' up a storm in English. I ask him about it, and he said he couldn't get anything done for all the snakes. It was like a family reunion. He repeated he couldn't get anything done for effect. I asked why he didn't cuss in Navajo, and he told me English had a lot better cuss words."

"That's funny."

"Yeah, it is. Hey, looks like we're here, Harmony Farms. Let's hope the owner's in a good mood."

Roger took a right on a farm lane that was well worn, with a few potholes containing muddy water and a small grassy strip down the middle. He pulled up to a parking area near a small building, and they got out. The air was thick with the smell of horses, and one whinnied from a nearby building. He heard a screen door close, and a large woman came around the block building. She looked to be about forty, and her skin was leathery from the sun. Could this be Mrs. Porcher's daughter? She was built like a refrigerator with a head. She wore a grubby T-shirt that covered two large saggy breasts unrestrained by a bra, and some well-worn blue jeans. An Aussie bush hat sat on her head. A bulge in her check showed a chaw of tobacco. Her long black hair with streaks of gray was braided and reached where her butt should have been, but wasn't. Suspenders kept her pants from falling down, and she wore heavy work boots. And she also had a pistol in a holster at her side.

She looked at Roger with suspicion. "Sorry, we're closed. Come back tomorrow when we're open." She spat on the ground.

Roger said, "I'm looking for Bridget Porcher. I was told I could find her here. Do you know where I can find her?"

"Who wants to know, and why?"

Roger cleared his throat. "My name's Roger Pyles and I've been hired by her mother. It seems her Pekingese, Tricki Woo, has disappeared, and I've been tryin' to find him for her. He seems to be headin' this way. I don't mean any trouble. I'm just tryin' to locate a lost dog."

She gave him the one over. "So, Tricki Woo's gone on walkabout, again."

"He has."

"And you said your name was what?"

"Roger Pyles."

"Roger Pyles," she repeated. "Wasn't there an article in Florida Today newspaper about you solving some kind of crime recently?"

160

"That would be me."

"You're better looking that the picture in the paper."

"Thank you. Seems like they always find a bad one to use. Either you've got a funny expression on your face or your mouth's wide open."

She laughed. "Very true. At least you've got something to work with." She paused. "I'm Bridget Porcher. So Tricki's on the lam again? How long's he been gone this time?"

"Two-three days. Could be four. No more. Your mother somehow heard I do detective and investigative work, probably from the paper, and contacted me. She and her driver showed up at my trailer in Canaveral Flats askin' for help findin' Tricki Woo."

"No kidding? My hoity-toity mother lowered herself to go slumming in Canaveral Flats to find you? Well, I'll be damned." She chucked. "She must be desperate."

Roger wasn't sure if it was time to grab Carlos and run for the hills or not, but she smiled. "Well, Mr. Roger Pyles. How about we have a seat in the shade and discuss this matter?"

"Okay."

"And who's this handsome young fellow you've got with you?"

"That's my son, Carlos."

"Hi," he said weakly.

She smiled. "No need to be shy, young man." She turned her attention to Roger. "Is it okay if someone shows him around while we talk? I have a lot of animals that would interest him."

"I guess so."

She turned to the building and yelled, "Hey, Emily, I need you. Come on out."

A young girl called out, "Okay." The sound of a screen door slamming against a wooden jamb could be heard, and a mixed-race girl about the same age as Carlos came around the corner. "What do you want?"

Bridget said, "Could you show this young man," she pointed to Carlos, "around while I talk to his dad?"

"Sure." Her eyes twinkled, and she motioned to him. "Come with me."

He smiled, and they ran to the barn and disappeared.

Bridget turned to Roger. "They'll have fun while we talk. Now, what can I do to help you, Roger? Is it just about the dog or has my mother included a covert operation?"

Chapter 31

"First off, Miss Bridget, my only interest is findin' your mother's lost dog. I know she will ask me about you, and I'll tell her what I saw, nothing more unless you have something for me to pass on to her." Roger read suspicion in her eyes. "She said Tricki had found his way here on one of his jaunts."

"That he did. Got two of my bitches knocked up, he did. He's quite a stud that Tricki. After the puppies were weaned, I had my little girls fixed. So, he's on the prowl, is he? He won't be getting any satisfaction here."

"We think he may be heading this way. My son saw a loose Pekingese over by the Waffle House, but he got away and our ability to search the area was limited by circumstances. The dog may or may not have been Tricki. Your mother sure misses her Tricki Woo. She calls me several times a day, askin' for updates."

"That sounds like my mom."

"I'm usually tryin' to track down some criminal, so lookin' for a lost dog is a little out of my normal work, but your mother can be quite persuasive. She sure wants him back."

She grunted. "If she'd treated us as well, we might get along better."

"Bridget, your mom seems like a lonely old lady. I'm just tryin' to get her dog back and make her happy."

Bridget seemed to be contemplating what he'd said. She sighed. "I hope she gets Tricki back, but he ain't here. If he shows up, I'll let you know."

"Thank you." He handed her a poster.

"Yeah, that's Tricki. Still got that grin on his face like he did after frolicking with the girls."

"Interesting place you have here, Miss Bridget."

"When my dad died, his will stipulated that me and my brother got a share of the estate at that time. I got this beat-up old farm, and he got a small house out 520 west of the interstate. Also, he left some money in a trust, and we get some interest off it each month. It's not a whole lot, but you can live on it if you have to. Mom's not happy with either of us, so I'm not sure she'll leave any of her estate to us when she passes.

"I've been trying to fix it up a little at a time as I can afford it. The horse barn was a dream for a long time, and I finally was able to get it built a little over a year ago. We board horses for people and have started an equestrian rescue. I'm working on a program to get handicapped children on horses. Gives you a good feeling to see the smiles on the kid's faces."

Roger said, "Do you take donkeys?"

"No, not even if my brother was brought in. Why do you ask?"

"I have a donkey foundling on my property. He showed up a while back, and it was either let him stay on my property or be put down. I said he could stay, but I'm still lookin' for a real home for him."

She sighed. "I've heard that story lots of times. Seems like there're lots of animals of all flavors in need of a home."

"Ain't that the truth?"

"The horse family includes horse, wild and domestic, large and small, zebras, and donkeys. They're very fascinating and about as diverse as the canine family. Mankind's been manipulating their form for as long as history's been written and before that."

Roger said, "What other animals do you have here?"

"It's like old McDonald's farm. A few pigs, a couple of pygmy goats, one emu, a llama, some rabbits that keep multiplying, but we eat them. A bunch of chickens for eggs, and of course a lot of horses. Tricki had some run-ins with the chickens when he was here. They don't like him, and he doesn't like them. He tried to get them, and they responded by pecking the living daylights out of him. I saw you looking at my gun. We have a lot of coyotes around here. Got a couple of my chickens."

"Yeah, I'm learnin' about coyote problems. Bridget, your mother said the two of you weren't on the best of terms. I don't need to know what the difficulties are. I know how it is with families. Something happens and then there's hurt feelings. She said not to even consider you as a suspect in Tricki's disappearance. Can you think of anyone that would want to take him? Would your brother possibly be of the mind to do so?"

She rubbed her chin that had a few long hairs sticking from it. "No, I can't think of anyone. Mom will drive a hard bargain, but I've never known her to take advantage of any party in her dealings. Now my brother, that's a different story. Hugh's not a bad guy, just lazy, never worked a day in his life if he could avoid it, likes to chase the skirts, and smoke weed all the time. Other than that, he's not a bad guy. No, I don't think he'd dognap Tricki."

Roger said. "I'd still want to visit him."

"Like I said, he lives west of the interstate off 520. Take a right on Osage Street and drive to the very end. He lives in the house at the very end when he's not shacked up with some hussy. You might get lucky and catch him there. And I don't have his phone number. He changes it so often, I can't keep up."

"Why so?"

"Jealous boyfriends and husbands. They get a little upset when they find he'd been fooling around with their women. Someday, one of them's going to shoot him for sure."

Roger said, "Thanks for the info. Anything else you'd like to tell me? If your mom's dog isn't here, there's no point in staying."

She sighed. "How's Mom?"

"A tough old lady, but lonely."

"I'm not surprised. She has a way of driving people away from her. She wanted me to be the perfect Southern Belle, a real debutante, but can you see me as a dainty little doll? I never had the body or the temperament for it, and she kept trying to turn me into what she wanted, something I could never be. I found my place in life here with my critters. I feel sorry for her sometimes." She looked off to the horizon. "Funny how opposites attract. My dad loved to work hard and get dirty while doing it. He was a hands on kind of guy. She thought he should be the boss man, sit in the office and tell people what to do, but that wasn't dad. Her nagging finally drove him into the arms of another woman."

"Why are you telling me this? Roger said.

"It's complicated, but you need to know some of the family dynamics. You see, Emily's my half-sister. When my mom found out about it, she went ballistic. Dad moved out and took up with Lawanna in the house my brother lives in. He came home one day and found the house robbed and her raped and murdered. Pop knew who had done it, a shady character in the neighborhood. He caught him at home, found some of his stuff there, shot the man six times with a 9mm pistol, and then went out into the street screaming he had nothing to live for. Then he shot himself in the head."

The thousand mile look came to her eyes again. "They wanted to put the baby in foster care. I know what a rotten deal that can be for a child. I petitioned the court to get Emily, and they agreed. She's why my Mom doesn't like to come here. Emily reminds her of the sorrow in her heart she tries to hide. I wish she could just move on and accept me and Emily for what we are, especially Emmy. She's such a good girl. Got a heart of gold she does, and sharp as a tack."

Tears started to roll down Bridget's face. She put her hands to her face and began to cry and then almost wail. Roger got up and went to her. He put his arm around her as she cried.

"It'll be alright. It will all work out," he said. "Somehow, it will work out. I know it will."

She sniffed. "I wish I could believe that. Thank you for your comfort, but what would you know of pain?"

Roger stepped away. "I've known of pain as black as the deepest prison in the deepest hole in the depths of this world. I've known what it feels like to have your heart ripped out and run through a shredder. I've known of hopelessness so bad I would have welcomed death itself. I know what it's like to hurt."

She nodded her head. "Well, perhaps you can try to tell my mom of a little of this for me. I'd appreciate that."

"I'll do what I can. If you see Tricki, give me a call, please."

She said, "I'll do that."

Emily and Carlos appeared. He yelled, "Dad, they got all kinds of neat animals!"

The adults turned to them and Emily and Carlos' faces fell. "Dad, are you okay?

Emily said to Bridget, "What wrong? You face is wet."

Bridget sniffed. "Got a bug in my eye. Give me a minute. I'll be okay."

Roger said. "It's okay, but we need to be goin'. You can tell me all about it in the truck."

"Mom," Emily said, "You sure you're okay?"

Bridget nodded, pulled a handkerchief from her pocket, and loudly blew her nose. "Yeah, I'm alright. Roger, it was good to talk with you. Remember what I said and please pass it on."

"I will. Carlos, we need to get back to searchin' for Tricki. Ready?"

"Sure. Nice to meet you, Emmy."

"I hope to see you again, Carlos. Bye."

Roger and Carlos walked to the truck. As he drove down the dirt road, he glanced in the rearview mirror and saw the two females waving goodbye. Carlos was also looking in his mirror and saw them. He rolled the window down, stuck his arm and head out, and waved.

Roger smiled. This visit sure had its surprises. Wonder if he really would find Tricki? He hoped so. Just like life, being a pet detective had its unexpected revelations. What more curveballs would life throw his way today? Maybe an epiphany? Unlikely, but you never know.

Chapter 32

"Why was she crying, Dad?"

"She wasn't cryin'. She had a bug in her eye."

Carlos said, "She was crying."

Roger grimaced. "Okay, she was cryin'."

"Why?"

"Adult stuff."

"Adult stuff?" Carlos said, "Mom says that sometimes when I ask her a question. I hate it when she does that. Makes me feel like a baby."

Roger thought for a suitable reply. "You'll understand when you got kids of your own."

Carlos glanced at his father. "I hope I never say that to my kids."

"Trust me, son, I thought the same thing when I was your age and reacted the same way. Funny how we grow up and become our parents."

Carlos was silent for a moment. "Emily was nice. She showed me the whole place and all the animals. It was neat."

"I bet it was. You didn't see Tricki Woo, did you?"

"No, but I saw his love interest, a little beagle. She had big floppy ears and a white tip on her tail. Emily said they had her fixed after Tricki had his way with her."

Roger laughed. "Tricki's been a busy guy."

"Where we going now?"

"Over to see Bridget's brother, Mrs. Porcher's son. I want you to stay in the truck."

"Why?"

"He sounds like a lowlife, and I don't want you exposed to that. Just stay in the truck. I shouldn't be long."

"Okay. Got anything to read?"

Roger said, "Think there might be a cowboy western under the seat. Check and see."

Carlos reached under the seat and pulled out a yellowed paperback. "Found one. Louis L'Amour. *The Sacketts*. Is it any good?"

"Why, he's the best. I think you'll like him. Hope it's not too hard to read."

"Dad, I learned to read when I was four. Teacher said I was a protégé, whatever that is."

"It means you're very smart."

"I thought so. How far we got to go?"

Roger said, "Not far."

They took a left on State Route 520, cruised under Interstate 95, and a mile later, turned left on Osage Street, and then drove to the end of the street. He saw the house Bridget had described and pulled into the driveway next to a '68 Ford Mustang. The house needed paint and a new roof, but the chain-link fenced yard looked almost respectable.

"Wait here while I go talk to Bridget's brother. I'll leave the AC on. Lock the doors and honk the horn if you need me," Roger said.

"Okay, Dad."

Roger heard the door locks click as he walked to the house. He turned his head and saw Carlos with his head in the book. *Good, that'll keep him busy.* He knocked on the door.

"Come on in," a male voice yelled. "Door's not locked."

Roger swung it open and saw a man plopped down in an overstuffed chair. He was clad only in gaudy tight shorts, had tattoos on his shoulders, and from the smell in the room, was smoking marijuana heavily.

"You ain't Leo," he said. "Why ain't you Leo? I was expecting him."

"Don't know no Leo. I'm Roger Pyles. I work for your mother."

"Well, ain't that interesting? Want a joint to smoke?"

"No. I'm here on business."

"What kind of business? Got something good to sell me? I could use a lid."

Roger said, "No lids and nothing to smoke. I'll lookin' for a lost dog, Tricki Woo."

"Aw, man. Don't be a party pooper. Smoke one. Loosen up a little."

"No, I'm here strictly on business. Are you Hugh?"

Hugh seemed disappointed with Roger.

Roger said, "Nice car you got out there."

Hugh's face lit up. "Yeah, my pride and joy. It's one like Steve McQueen drove in the movie, *Bullitt*. It'll kick butt just like his did in the chase scene through San Francisco."

"I bet it will."

"But I got to chill it now. Got too many tickets from the man. One more and I lose my license. I keep it around 'cause it's such a chick magnet. Lose my license and I'm up the creek big time. Can't have that. Sure you don't want a joint?"

"No, for the third time. I'm a LEO, Law Enforcement Officers."

"Hugh said, "Not my friend Leo, but a LEO? You're a cop? Where's your badge?'

Roger winced. "I don't have it with me."

Hugh smiled. "Right. Well. Mr. LEO without a badge. What do you want then?"

"I told you. I'm workin' for your mother and lookin' for her Pekingese."

"Mom hired a pet detective to find Tricki? You got a license to do this? She must be desperate."

"No, I don't have a license, and she wants him back bad. There's a reward, too. No questions asked. Here's a poster I made."

"Thanks. How big is the reward?"

"Big enough. You got him?"

Hugh said, "No. Wish I did. I could always use the bread. Being a Casanova ain't cheap. Chicks like to have a good time, you know what I mean?"

Roger said, "Yeah, I know what you mean. If Tricki's not here, there's no reason for me to remain here."

"Sure you don't want to burn one?"

"No. Thinkin' I'm gettin' a contact high just bein' here."

Hugh smiled. "Yeah, it's good stuff. Nothin' but the best."

"Call me at the number if you see him, okay? I'm leavin'. Bye."

"Bye."

Hugh watched as Roger got in his truck and drove away.

So, Tricki Woo was missing. Took off again when he got lusty, I bet. I can understand that. Hope he shows up here. I could use the money. Wonder where he is?

Chapter 33

Roger got in his truck and exhaled. He shook his head.

"Pretty bad, Dad?"

"Yeah, it was. About what I expected."

"You smell funny."

"Not surprised. He was smokin' a lot of high power weed."

"Marijuana?"

Roger said, "Yeah, what do you know about marijuana?"

"Mom says to stay away from it. It's bad for you. Someone in the neighborhood was smoking it, and the wind carried the smell our way. She told me what it was when I asked."

"It's illegal. People waste a lot of their lives smokin' that stuff, and think they're really livin'. There're a lot of ways to ruin one's life. I know."

Carlos seemed to contemplate that thought for a moment. "Where we going now?"

"Grocery shoppin'. Don't that sound like fun?"

"Sure beats starving."

"It does. Most people don't know where our food comes from."

"Publix or Winn Dixie."

Roger said, "I would expect you to say that being only eight."

"I'll be nine real soon. Mom says I'm growing up too fast."

"I agree with her on that one. Let me tell you a story about a gallon of milk. It gets shipped in by a truck from a distribution center the grocery store has. Once at the store it has to be unloaded and put in a cooler so you can find it. You pay for it, as you know and carry it home. A lot of people are involved in the whole process. As the price of fuel goes up and down, it impacts the price of food and that impacts how much money we have to spend on other things.

"It starts all the way back at a dairy farm where a farmer has to have a big herd of cows, girls of course, he cares for by feeding and keepin' them healthy. You can't get milk from a bull no matter how hard you try. He has machinery that milks them. The milk is then sent to a processing plant in a big tanker truck. Then the milk is heated to kill any germs, and then cooled to preserve it. Next it gets separated into cream and skim milk. Every item containin' milk uses those two items."

Carlos said, "Like ice cream?"

"Like ice cream."

"I like ice cream."

Roger said, "You wouldn't be wantin' some, would you?"

Carlos smiled.

"I thought so."

"Chocolate is my favorite."

"The store should have that and other flavors, too. Now, getting back to the milk story. At the processing plant, people inspect it for safety. People have gotten sick from drinkin' bad milk. Then they package it, send it to the grocery story distribution center, and you know the rest."

"Sounds complicated."

Roger said. "It is, and I'm givin' you the simplified version. And I may have gotten a few things out of order, but that's the basic story. It is rather complicated because of a lot more factors I didn't mention. Like what if the grocery store can't find workers. What if they can't get to work because there's no gas to put in their cars, or it's too expensive to buy? Want to hear more?"

"No. you're making my head hurt. I get it. It's complicated."

"A lot more than your average Joe, or politician, or citizen would know. I think the worst are the know it all college kids. They get a degree and think they know everything. I would know. I've been around a lot of them when I was a college professor up north."

Carlos said, "Why did you leave?"

"I found I was no longer welcome because I dared to disagree with the establishment. They called themselves a university which means they educate students with all facts and information available, so they will be knowledgeable and wise, supposedly. When I did that, they tried to run me out. It seemed only certain information was allowed to reach the young student's minds. Fortunately, some people stuck with me, and I came out of it with compensation. My wife and son, your half-brother, died about that time, and I moved here to get away from my problems, or so I hoped."

"That's a long sad story."

Roger said, "There's more, but I'll spare you that till another time."

"Thanks. Dad, why do you do cop stuff?"

"I started when I was up north teachin'. One of the local cops thought my skills might be useful to an investigation they were doin'. It was, and they kept askin' for my help. I was good at it and enjoyed it for the most part. I found I had a real sense of justice. I wanted to bring some into an unjust world. Make it better."

"Mom says some of the same things, but I think she sometimes gets frustrated."

"Can't say I blame her. It happens to a lot of people in police work. They see the same people over and over and wonder if they're makin' a difference or fightin' a battle they can't win."

Carlos said. "What do you think?"

"I think I understand why they feel that way. I do, too, sometimes. The world is such a big place, and I'm only one, but I do what I can to try to make it better and just. That's the best answer I can give. Got any more questions?'

"Mom says I'm full of questions."

"Good. People full of questions want answers, to be well informed. Maximilien Robespierre once said, 'The secret to freedom lies in educating people, whereas the secret to tyranny is in keeping them ignorant.'"

"Who?"

"Some old French philosopher with some radical ideas, some good and some not so good during the French Revolution, and as radical revolutions often go, he became a victim. They whacked off his head."

Carlos flinched.

"If you have any more questions, I'm afraid they'll have to wait. I'm about to turn into the grocery store parkin' lot. Hold any questions till later. And none will make me want to whack off your head. Got that?"

"Got it. Shut up, but only if you promise to get ice cream."

"Are you pushin' your luck? Am I raisin' a little scoundrel? Don't answer that. No bribery necessary. We are gettin' ice cream and a bunch of other things. Man shall not live on ice cream alone."

"Super. Thanks, Dad."

After finding a suitable spot under a shade tree, they walked into the store, found a buggy with a wobbly wheel, of course, and began shopping. Roger's phone rang. He looked at the number, Mrs. Porcher. Someone wanted an update. Maybe she had information for him, too.

Chapter 34

"Got a call from Mrs. Porcher, Carlos. Let's go outside. The phone reception should be better."

"But it's hot out there, Dad. I don't want to go back out in the heat. You're getting service right here."

"It's not very good. Let's go to the front of the store by the windows. Should be a better signal there."

"Okay."

Roger made small talk with Mrs. Porcher as they walked there. Sure enough, the reception was better.

"Yes, Mrs. Porcher. I've been busy. Any news for me from your end? No more nasty visitors?" Pause. "That's good. I'm in Port St. John at the Winn Dixie grocery shoppin'. Phone reception is pretty bad. Don't be surprised if the call drops." Pause. "Have I any good news for you? Well, Tricki is still missing. I visited your daughter and son at their places. No sign of him at either place. The little girl who lives with your daughter showed Carlos all the sights on the little farm but saw no Tricki Woo. Your son was all smoked up and seemed interested when I mentioned the reward. He seemed not to know that Tricki was on the lam.

"Yes, he was a little more than I expected, even from your description of him. I practically had to cut through the haze with a knife to get through. Yes, let's remain hopeful. Tricki has impressed me as a little resourceful dog who can take care of himself. Given enough time, I think he will turn up. He's probably gettin' tired by now, and thinkin' of the good life he had with you. Yes, Mrs. Porcher, I'll let you know when I have new information about him. Bye."

Roger disconnected the call.

"Dad, she seemed anxious and worried from what little I could hear."

"Yeah, she is. She definitely wants him back in a bad way. I sure hope this all ends well for her. I'm beginnin' to like the little fella, even though I've never seen him."

"How do you think K9 is doing?"

Roger said, "Still improvin', I hope. Let's get our shoppin' done quickly, go home, and see."

Carlos nodded.

"Roger," a voice cried out.

He turned his head and saw Chief of Police Bill Kenney coming his way. "Well, what do you want, you old scudder?"

"Hey, you resemble that term as much as I do. How's the dog hunt going?"

Roger said, "Not so good. A possible sighting down by the Waffle House in Cocoa along I 95. No luck at the animal shelters either. I rounded up the usual suspects but have little to show for it. Still, I have this feelin' it will all work out."

Bill nodded. "I hope so. It's been a quiet day in Lake Wobegon. I like those kinds of days. I stopped at your place and did a wellness check on your dog. She got up, growled at me, so I know she's feeling better."

Roger smiled. "That sounds like the old K9 we know and love. If she growled at you, we know she's feelin' better."

Bill laughed and spoke to Carlos. "Have you been keepin' your dad out of trouble?"

"Yeah, we've been investigating the missing dog together. I may want to be a cop when I grow up."

Bill said, "You'll have lots of time to figure out what you want to be as you grow up." He turned his attention to Roger. "I have some things I need to speak with you about, but not here in this public place. How about I stop over after I'm done shopping and discuss it with you?"

"Sounds good. I got shoppin' to do, too. Kid's goin' to eat me out of house and home."

"By the way, a realtor was out putting up signs for the property next to you and across the street. I spoke with him about the prices the owners were asking. They sounded very reasonable. He said they were motivated to sell and would accept any reasonable offer. He said he thought they would sell pretty quick, so if you're interested, you better get on the stick and do something before they're gone. Here's his business card."

Roger took the card. "Thanks, Bill, for both bits of information."

"You know me. We aim to serve."

"Yeah, I know you alright. Just the same, thanks again."

Bill said, "Then I'll see you later, gator." He pulled a buggy from the rack and headed for the bakery section.

"Well, young man, let's get to work."

Carlos said, "Looking at all this food and smelling all these good smells is making me hungry."

"Me, too, and that can be a bad thing. You tend to buy more than you need when you're hungry, and I have limited space, not that I need a whole lot, but I seem to keep addin' more mouths all the time. First K9, then the cat, then Donkey, and now you showed up."

"You're like a magnet, Dad."

He smiled. "Guess I am. Let's get some shoppin' done."

They went to the right side of the store and began. Thirty minutes later, the cart was more full than empty, and they headed for the check-out. It started to rain as they walked to the truck. Roger piled the bags on the floor and on the seat where Carlos normally would have sat and he rode next to his dad as they went home. It rained heavily as they drove down US 1 but let up as they turned onto Canaveral Flats Boulevard. Its large potholes were full of sandy-colored water. They bounced along. Carlos had to stop one bag from falling over. The rain stopped by the time they reached Roger's trailer, but water stood in low spots on his and the lot next to him that was for sale.

They carried the bags in and found spots for most of the food on the small amount of shelving he had. One-half gallon of ice cream and the frozen dinners took up most of the small freezer in the top of the refrigerator.

"Looks like we're gonna have to eat about half that ice cream. I can cut the box down and make it fit if we do," Roger said. "Do you think we can handle it, marine?"

Carlos smiled and saluted. "Yes, sir. We can handle it."

"Good. What was I thinkin'? We'll eat the TV dinners and then have space for the ice cream. We won't have to eat it at all."

Carlos' face fell.

"Just kiddin'. We'll eat what we want, but not enough to make us sick or get a brain freeze."

"Pop, you're the best."

Roger smiled inside. Maybe God was showing undeserved favor on the wretch Roger sometimes felt like. Maybe He was giving him a second chance at parenthood. Roger didn't want to screw it up and let this chance slip through his fingers. He grinned. Maybe it would work out. He slipped a dinner into the microwave oven and set the timer. A sound outside caught his attention. Bill Kenney was coming down the driveway in his truck.

Wonder what he has to tell me that's so all fired up important? Guess I'll soon find out.

Chapter 35

Bill pulled his truck up beside Roger's and got out. "Hey, stranger, long time no see."

K9 got up and growled.

Roger said, "Looks like my intruder alert is feeling better."

"I told you so. I'm glad to see things are returning to normal. Permission to come aboard, Captain."

"Get in here, you big galoot. You usually just barge in here like you own the place, grab one of my beers, and plop down on the furniture. Why the change?"

"Part of the kinder, gentler me. Either that or I'm getting old."

Roger laughed. "I'm heatin' up TV dinners for me and Carlos. Want one?"

"No, Suzie invited me to supper. It was good and tasty. She's some cook, that cousin of yours."

"She's never invited me to supper, but I'm glad you ate. I only had two TV dinners. My trailer's refrigerator isn't very big."

Bill said, "You ought to think about buying the properties I told you about. Seems like you're gonna stay. You could use a real house to make a home for you, not this metal box."

"You got a point there. I am startin' to like this place, but I still like my mountain home."

"We call it getting sand in your shoes. Hey, the mountains will still be there when they beckon and call you from Almost Heaven, West Virginia."

"Guess you're right," Roger said. "Still need a beer?"

"Sure. Thanks."

Roger went inside and returned with a twelve-ounce Yuenglings in his hand and passed it to Bill.

"Thanks." He twisted the top off and took a big sip. "That was good."

"Need another? You're not on duty, are you?"

"Yes, I could use another, and no, I'm not on duty."

Roger pulled a bottle from his back pocket and gave it to Bill, who nodded a thank you as he gulped his first beer.

Bill said, "Ah, that was good. Why are you being so generous today?"

Roger grinned. "I needed the space in the frig, and Carlos's already heatin' the second TV dinner." A bell rang. "Looks like it's done. I figured a second beer would keep you content while we ate."

"You figured right. Enjoy your meal with your son. I'll wait."

Roger went inside and found Carlos had the meals on the table with a napkin and plastic ware next to them. He'd poured tea for both of them.

"Wow, that looks good. I'm beginnin' to like this family thing."

"Mom taught me to do this when she's at work or busy. Sometimes I get hungry before she does."

"Good for you. Glad to see she's tryin' to raise your right." He sat down and started eating.

Carlos looked at him strangely. "Aren't you gonna say a prayer, give thanks? Mom always says I should be thankful for my food. Many people aren't as blessed around the world."

"She's right. Glad she's tryin' to do the right thing. Guess she would know, too, from the stories her dad, your granddad, must have told her about livin' in Cuba." He paused. "Dear Lord, thank You for all this grub on our table, this abundance to share with family. Amen. Was that good enough?"

"Yeah, it'll do. Let's eat. I'm hungry."

And so they did. The dinners were tasty, especially after adding salt, pepper, and some Tabasco sauce. They ate quickly and threw the containers in the trash.

Carlos said, "I'll wash the utensils and cups, and you can talk with Mr. Bill. I want to read my Jungle Book."

"Good stories from Rudyard Kipling. I liked Elephant's Child."

"That's my next one to read."

"You'll enjoy it. Now, let me see what my ole scalawag of a friend wants."

"Sure, Dad."

Roger grabbed two beers and went outside. He handed one to Bill. "This won't put you over the line, will it?"

"Don't think so. Thanks."

Roger sat down and reclined in his La-Z-Boy chair. "Okay, Bill, what's on your mind besides the properties for sale?"

"Several things."

Bill opened his mouth to speak, but was shut down by Carlos, who yelled from the trailer door, "Can I polish off a bunch of ice cream, Dad?"

"Do something constructive. Clean out some more space in the freezer."

"Huh?"

"Yeah, help yourself to the ice cream. Just don't make yourself sick eating too much."

"Okay. Why didn't you say so?" Carlos shut the door, listening to the two men laughing.

Roger said, "Sorry about that. His manners need worked on."

"Don't we all?"

Bill said, "You better make sure he knows we were just having a little fun with him. Don't want to hurt his feelings."

Roger said, "Good thought. I'll make sure I do. I have a question for you. How's your investigation into the vote fraud in the county goin?"

"I've gone about as far as I can go. I'll turn in my report, Hope something happens, but I doubt much will. Still, this is not the end of it. I know there's more there. That vehicle going into the pond was a stroke of luck. Finding those disposed of boxes of legal ballots has shown a little light on a practice that I believe may go back to the days of Reconstruction and even before. I found historical records that during the election of 1864 in New York City, the Copperhead groups operating there, tried to steal the election away from Lincoln using fraudulent mail-in absentee votes. It's kept political parties in power for decades. Some of their techniques have changed, but the desired outcome has not. Absentee ballots are the tools of choice for fraud because they're easy to steal, alter, and forge. Voter rolls are often inaccurate and outdated containing names of dead people, some who have moved, and no longer eligible for a number of reasons. He who controls and counts the votes wins the election. Boy, have I got an education on the subject."

Roger nodded.

"Just like on the ocean, you can tell something's not right under the surface. You can feel it, but only catch little glimpse of the problem. It's like seeing a little smoke from the smoking gun, but never finding the gun. They've had time to learn how to hide it and keep it hidden."

"That's not very promising," Roger said.

"No, it's not, but it's a start. Some of the old establishment has a little fear in their eyes. They're afraid this will become common knowledge they'll try to deny, and it will be their downfall."

"So, where do we go from here?"

Bill said, "I put some recommendations in my findings. We have to be proactive. As the old folks say, an ounce of prevention is worth a pound of cure. We need to fix the system before voting happens. It's far easier to do that than let the cheaters cheat and then try to prove they did it when they already control the outcome. First, we need to get the word out. Rats don't like the light of day."

"How you gonna do that?" Roger said.

"It will be difficult seeing the power brokers are in bed with the newspapers and media people, but it can be done with grass root efforts. Second, the voter files must be cleaned out. I found lots of problems. People 125 years of age voting. Numerous people voting from a vacant lot. I bet at least 10% of the people on the role aren't eligible to vote. They don't meet the minimum qualifications. I found evidence of dark money flowing into the county to influence the election. We need eyes on every ballot to insure all legal votes are counted. Integrity is paramount. All ballots must be secure from the polling place, to where they are counted, and throughout the count, and finally in the reporting. Questionable ballots cannot just show up in the middle of the night and be counted if we ever want to have a clean and fair election."

"That sounds like a tall order."

Bill said, "It is, but I think it's worth it. I'm like you. I want justice and what's best for our citizens. Our nation needs free and fair elections we can trust. The wool's been pulled over our eyes too many times."

Roger nodded. "Okay, what more did you need to tell me?"

"Several things. I got some information you need to know…"

"Stop right there," Roger said. "I know that, but I have one more simple question. There's something I need to know." He posed as Bill shifted in his chair. "Did you and K9 get along okay while you were waitin' on me?"

Bill sighed. "We did. She only growled a little. I told her I forgave her for the mess she made in my truck when we first got her. Guess anyone or anything can get sick in the worst way. Nobody is calling me stinky anymore, fortunately. The dog diarrhea all over my truck seems to be a story being forgotten," Bill said.

"So, she understood all of that?"

"As well as she could. I spoke to her gently and calmly. I thought I even saw a little wag of her tail before she crawled under the trailer and went to sleep. I heard her snoring. I think you woke her up, but she went back to sleep."

Roger said, "That's good. I'd hate for her to get sick biting you."

"Very funny, old friend. Do you want to hear what I came over to talk with you about or not? I don't need to stay here and be insulted even after three beers have mellowed me out."

"Want another? I'm still wondering when you're gonna get to what's on the tip of your tongue?"

"No, I've reached the limit, but thanks." He stopped. "Word travels fast. I heard about the bodies that were found today down at the Cocoa Waffle House and further south. FYI, this isn't the first time it's happened. Been a bunch of them turning up from here to Palm Bay. Young women, prostitutes, runaways, at least the ones we've been able to identify. Lots are still listed as Jane Does. I'm not the only one who thinks we have a serial killer operating in the county."

191

"That's pretty heavy-duty information," Roger said. "Why are you tellin' me?"

"There's scuttlebutt talk about naming a special investigator, and your name is top on the list."

"Serious?"

"As a heart attack. I think you're just the man for the job and told the Sheriff so."

Roger said, "Thanks for the vote of confidence, but I'm workin' a case."

"The dog will turn up, or he won't. How's it going, anyway?"

"After the last case, it's a welcome break. I needed it. Findin' my people skills are gettin' a workout tryin' to find Tricki Woo."

"How so?" Bill asked.

"Everyone wants to see my badge when I'm at a crime scene, and I ain't got one. That stoner of a son of Mrs. Porcher gave me a hard time, as did others. He even wanted to see my pet detective license."

"Ain't no such thing in this state."

Roger said, "I know that now, but I need an official badge if I'm gonna work this kind of work."

"I know her son. Had a run-in with him. Caught him and a filly doing the backseat boogie on a side road here in the Flats. He was all smoked up or drunk or both. I told them to get dressed and get out of here. Get a motel. She was fit to drive, so he gave her the keys, and it was good riddance. I don't think he's such a bad guy, irresponsible, but not bad. Just likes to party. If we locked up everyone like him, the jail would be more full and overflowing than it already is. Gonna have to add more beds as the county grows, whether we want to or not." He stopped. "I'll talk with Mayor Lester about getting you a badge. Happy?"

A broad, toothy smile came to Roger's face. "That would make me very happy. The sooner the better."

"Consider it done."

"You said there were things, as in plural you wanted to talk with me about. What else?"

"I think I may be having romantic feelings about your cousin Suzie."

"Oh Lord, have mercy. You guys ain't moved in together and shackin' up, are you? You're finally gettin' to what's been ruminatin' in your craw."

"No. I told you I don't mix business and pleasure," Bill said.

"Does she know?"

"Yeah, she does. And I think it's mutual, and that scares me. I've always been footloose and fancy-free. Love 'em and leave 'em. You know the drill, but this just feels different. Could this old bachelor be falling in love?"

Roger put his hand to his chin and sighed. "Could be."

"Are you okay with that?"

"Bill, I'm a little surprised. She was in a real mess, a real pickle, when she showed up a while back. I was worried about her. I've noticed she seemed to have adjusted well to her new status in life."

"So, is it okay if I date her?"

"Why are you askin' me? She's a grown woman. You ask her. This ain't no John Smith-Pocahontas thingy. Ask her yourself. Just don't mistreat her. She is family, you know."

Bill said, "I wouldn't think of it. I was just surprised by your concern about her after some of those stories she told me of those tricks you played on her when you guys were young."

Roger grinned. "Yeah, I was kinda rough on her, but when you're a young boy with an annoyin' girl cousin in the house. It was a lot of fun to tease her and get her goin'. Did she ever tell you about the time I-"

"I don't want to hear it. She can tell me, if and when, she wants to."

"Probably better that way. You two just play nice and see if anythin' develops. I'm good with it. Can I give you some free advice, and you know what they say about free advice."

Bill said, "Sure, I'll consider the source."

"You and I have been around the pike when it comes to women. And neither of us is perfect, especially when alcohol is involved. You know about the love 'em and leave 'em. You said you and Suzie haven't been messin' around. Don't. It's better with one woman, a wife you truly love. I loved my late wife, Kay. You ask how could it be better with the same woman, but she wasn't the same woman, and I wasn't the same man. We both changed over time. We grew as people, and our love grew with time. Our intimacy got better. It was like a fine wine that matured over time. It was a bond that grew and strengthened. Oh, how I'd love to find another woman to enjoy those white-hot coals of enduring intimacy over occasional flashes of passion. It's so much better when based on love and not lust."

"You surprise me sometimes. Thank you, Roger, for your understanding and candor."

Roger said, "Yeah, I don't know what's getting' into me, either."

"I better go."

"Anything more?"

"No. Just remember what I said about the proposed investigation. Think about it if you want it. It could be a lot of work and could lead you nowhere. Cases like this can be hard to crack."

Roger said, "Just the kind I like. Thanks for the heads up."

The two men rose from their chairs and shook hands.

"Be seeing you, Roger."

"Okay, Bill. Thanks for the heads up. And don't mess with Suzie."

"I wouldn't think about it. Bye."

Roger watched Bill's truck disappear down Canaveral Flats Boulevard. He'd had his suspicions about something going on between the two of them, but it had been a surprise he was being considered for a case of that magnitude by the county. Life has its surprises for sure. And where was Tricki Woo? Where in the world was he, and what was he up to?

Chapter 36

Tricki Woo was having the time of his life. His adventure continued. Places to go. Butts to sniff. He was getting more factual information from doing that then reading the newspaper, but he didn't know it.

He'd encountered numerous other dogs along the way. Most were friendly and wanted to play, but a few were not and he left quickly. No point in staying where he wasn't wanted or welcome. Several bitches were especially welcoming, and he spent extra time in their company. When they were both worn out and needed a rest, he left for greener pastures.

Speaking of pastures, he'd been chased by a cow and then a goat and finally some chickens. He hated chickens, and the feeling was mutual. He'd chase and nip at them, and they'd chase and peck at him. After a few pecks, he'd grow tired of the game and move on.

He'd tried to stay off the roads as much as possible on his way west, but canals and swampy areas gave him no choice but to travel along sections of highway, some paved, some not. Tricki'd seen some more of those dead logs with legs that came to life, and wanted to avoid them. A dead raccoon and also an armadillo in the road were interesting. He'd even eaten a chunk of the raccoon before a bunch of vultures flew in and threatened him with their menacing beaks. He wasn't sure what they were. Some kind of big chicken, and after remembering the chicken pecks, he wanted no part of this larger version. Maybe they were cousins of some sort, an even more rotten kind of chicken.

The roads were confusing. Some had been changed since he'd last been here, and there were new ones and new ditches to explore and avoid if possible. He spent the night in a thicket sleeping peacefully until a car full of teenage boys parked nearby. They got louder and louder until the blue lights appeared, and then they took off with blue lights in pursuit. After the night quiet returned, a young field rat, probably looking for a meal among the brambles, woke Tricki, who made quick work of him. The rat tasted good. He hadn't found much to eat since the piece of raccoon.

He wondered about Mrs. Porcher. Was she missing him? Most likely. He missed the large regular meals and the way she doted over him. His hairy fur was getting dirty and had some tangles. He missed his groomer. It always felt so good after she finished with him. Oh, well. He was on an adventure and roughing it. He'd manage, he knew. There was so much to do and see, and especially female company to enjoy. He'd be ready to return to Mrs. Porcher in time, but not yet.

Dawn came, and Tricki shook the dew from his coat. What's that? He smelled something putrid, and something good. Both interested him. It was time to explore. He knew what one odor was, but what was the other. He had to know, and maybe he'd even roll in it.

Chapter 37

Canaveral Flats

"That smells good," Roger said. He inhaled the steam rising from his coffee cup. *The Elixir of life. Nectar of the Gods. Ahh.*

"Woof."

"Yeah, I hear it, K9. Someone's comin' this way all bright and early. Ain't even hardly daylight yet. Wonder who it can be? Wrong direction to be goin' to work. Guess we'll soon find out, and they stopped in front of the gate. Looks like we got a visitor. Your friend or mine?"

"Woof."

"Yeah, I thought so. Looks like she's openin' the gate and letterin' herself in. At least, I think it's a she. Hard to see in this dim light. Small stature. Car and stature does look somewhat familiar."

Roger took another sip of his steaming coffee as the car approached his old trailer. "Gonna have to actually lock that gate, not dummy-lock it, if I want any privacy, K9."

The car stopped and a small woman got out. "Roger, could I come in?"

"Eva? Eva Egged? Is that you?"

"It's me."

"What are you doin' here at this hour of the morning? You must have woke up the roosters."

"I did, and they didn't like it."

Roger said, "Well, whatever it is, I'm sure it's important. Come on in. Cup of coffee?"

"Yes, please. Black is fine."

Roger got a cup from in the house. He found Eva sitting in a lawn chair eyeing K9. "Here's your coffee."

"Thank you."

"Don't mind K9. She won't hurt you."

"I didn't think so, but I still remember the dogs the guards at the prison camp had. Dogs can still frighten me."

Roger nodded. "Yeah, I can understand how that can be. It's all in how they were treated and raised."

She took a sip. "Good coffee."

"So what's up, Eva? I haven't seen you since the encounter with those Nazis, ODESSA branch, where we both almost died. What's up?"

"How much time do you have for a hurting old lady?"

"All the time in the world."

Roger thought he saw a tear roll down her cheek, but she tried to brush it away without his noticing.

She said, "Roger, I haven't slept since yesterday. I've been up all night reading. I got hungry and went to Denny's. You know it and Waffle House are about the only places to get a meal during the night."

"Yeah, lotta drunks go there after bar closing, get a meal, and try to sober up enough to drive home."

"I wasn't drunk. I was stone sober and wide awake. My day had been pretty normal. A little shopping, and then I went to the Catholic Thrift Store. I found a nice blouse, cheap too, and a picture I liked, but I was stopped dead in my tracks when I saw a book cover in the used book section. There she was. That face. I could never forget that face no matter how many years ago it was. It was her looking back at me with those same deep eyes."

"Who? Eva? Who?"

"Corrie Ten Boom. She was the Dutch woman I saw at the Ravensbrück Prison Camp. I could never forget those eyes. I had to have that book and immediately bought it."

"What's it called?" Roger said.

The Hiding Place. It tells the story of her life from a little girl growing up in Holland, the coming of the Nazis, hiding Jews from them, getting caught, imprisoned, watching her family die there, surviving, and somehow making a life afterward."

"I've heard the name. I think she died a few years ago."

Eva's face fell. "I would have liked so much to meet her. But still, I think I know her from her book."

"It definitely seems to have impacted you."

200

"It has. I was reading it sitting at Denny's. The waitress saw my book, business was slow, and so she started a conversation. She said it was a good book, and she got a lot out of it when she read it. I asked how so. She said she'd had a lot of troubles in her life, some self-inflicted she never wanted to do again, and the book had proven to her she, too, could overcome her difficulties if Corrie had. She looked like she'd had a hard life, was missing several teeth, but seems to have adjusted to her lot in life, and making the best of it."

Roger said, "Another Jew, Victor Frankl, who went through the Holocaust said something similar, 'When we are no longer able to change a situation, we are challenged to change ourselves.'"

"I know the name, but I'm not there. It's more like Robert Benson's book, *Between the Dreaming and the Coming True.* It says…I would rather we had died that day, than to have found ourselves here, lost somewhere between dreaming and coming true. That's how I feel today, Roger, stuck between the living and the dead."

"I know the feeling."

They sat in silence for a long moment.

Eva spoke, "She left me to my meal and book. I sat there sipping my coffee just reading for hours that seemed like minutes as Corrie spoke to my old dead heart. Roger, I was glad when Erica, that terrible person, jumped from the roof to her death. I even felt a little joy as I heard her body crash to the ground. It seemed like maybe, finally, some justice had been done."

She sniffed." I don't know how Corrie could forgive the Nazis for what they had done to her, but she did. It didn't happen overnight."

Eva sighed. "Corrie was let out of prison on a book-keeping error. It saved her life. Was it a mistake or a divine intervention? She seemed to think the latter, but I don't know. She went back to Holland and tried to help people, who like her, had lost everything. She traveled all over Europe sharing her message of God's forgiveness in places the war destroyed.

"In 1947, she went back to Germany. The war was too raw for many. After a meeting, solemn faces stared back at her unable to believe her message. That's when she saw him working his way right toward her from the crowd. He'd been a cruel guard at the prison her family was sent, and he was still wearing the army overcoat, brown hat, a blue uniform with its skull and crossbones. She wanted to run away. Her sister, Betsie and her had been forced to walk naked past this man. I may have, too. Oh, the shame, I could feel it firsthand.

"There he was in front of her with his hand thrust out. 'A fine message, fräulein! How good it is to know that our sins are at the bottom of the sea.' She couldn't take his hand, but fumbled it into her pocketbook. He wouldn't and didn't remember her, but she remembered him. 'You mentioned Ravensbrück. I was a guard there. I'm now a Christian. And I know God has forgiven me of all the cruel things I've done.' He stretched his hand out again. 'Fräulein-will you forgive me?'"

"She stood there as a coldness gripped her heart and unable to speak. She had to forgive. She knew it. The words of Jesus rang in her ears, 'If you do not forgive men their trespasses, neither will your Father in heaven forgive you.' She knew what she must do. Forgiveness is not an emotion, but an act of the will. She said, 'I forgive you, brother! With all my heart!' A healing warmth seemed to flow from her most inner most being. Never had she felt such peace.

"Roger, I've been nursing my bitterness. I don't think I can ever forgive them of what they did, but my heart is a little more open because of her powerful testimony that anything is possible."

Her sad, hopeful eyes met Roger's.

He nodded. "We all have to work at our own pace. I can understand completely. Let me tell you a story Pastor Nassey told me. 'There's a bell in a church tower. Once it's swung by the rope, you have to let go, but the bell still will continue to swing slower and slower until the final ding where it stops.

"He said forgiveness was like that. Take your hand off the rope. But if we've been yankin' on our grievances for a long, long time, don't be surprised if the old angry vengeful thoughts come back a while. The old bell is just slowing down, and you're hearing the final ding-dongs."

"Roger, I'm not there yet."

He put his arm around her. "I know, but you're makin' progress. You're learnin' to forgive."

Eva began to sob, and then the tears came like a flood. Her body convulsed as she cried. Roger held her tight as she cried for the longest time. She signed, sniffed, and rubbed the tears from her eyes. "Guess you think I'm just a silly, old woman?"

"No, Eva. I like you just the way you are, warts and scars and all. There'll never be another creature like you."

She sniffed again and took a sip of her coffee. "Cold."

"I'll get you a warmer-upper."

"No," she sighed. "You gave me what I really needed, a listening, concerned ear. That was worth more than all the gold of the world."

"Thank you, Eva. And coffee. Don't forget the coffee."

"Oh, you're such a jokester. You know just what I wanted and needed."

Roger smiled, "Just glad to be of service and help."

"You were wonderful, but I must be going. I feel more relaxed and I think I can get some much needed rest. Thank you, Roger. I'll never forget this."

"Nor I."

She got up. "Bye. Hope to see you again soon."

"Likewise, I'm sure."

Roger watched as her car disappeared east on Canaveral Flats Boulevard. A noise at the door started him. "Carlos, how long have you been there?"

"A while."

"How much did you hear?"

"Enough."

"That was confidential, understand. Not to be repeated."

"Thought so. I already forget whatever you were talking about."

"Good boy."

"I fixed up two microwave breakfasts. Hungry?"

Roger said, "Yeah, I am. I didn't hear the bell on it ring."

"Think it's broke."

"Could be. Let's eat."

After a short prayer, the hungry boys chowed down heartily. They gathered up the paper plates after finishing, and the cell phone rang.

"Looks like this is still working. Wonder who that is? Good news I hope?...Hey, Harmony Farms. Maybe it is good news. Hello?"

Chapter 38

"Bridget, it is good to hear from you. What's up?"

"Tricki Woo has surfaced?"

"That's great news. Is he at your place? He is? Good. How is he? Dirty. Needs a bath and a brushing. That's to be expected. Is he healthy?"

Roger smiled. "Too healthy. Doin' typical dog things like running through the barnyard, chasing your chickens, getting' pecked, and tryin' to hump your beagle. That sounds like the Tricki Woo we know and love."

"So, what do you want me to do? Uh-huh. Uh-huh. I think I can do that. I think your mother will agree to just about anything to get her precious dog back. Let's press our luck a little. Agreed. Okay, let's make it noonish. Bye."

Carlos looked at his father with inquiring eyes. "Well?"

"Tricki Woo had been found."

"Hurray. Long live Tricki." He stopped. "Now what?"

"Well, the obvious. We return him to his owner, but we want to heal some family wounds if we can. We want to try to make things better."

"How're we gonna do that, Dad?"

"By a little conning, cunning, and sleight of hand, if possible."

"Huh?"

"We give Mrs. Porcher what she wants and a little more she needs."

Carlos looked puzzled.

Roger smiled. "Can you trust me on this one?"

"Sure, Dad. I love it when a plan comes together."

"Sounds like your mom has been lettin' you watch *The A-Team.*"

He grinned. "She does. I like Mr. T and the gang."

Roger laughed. "Don't go thinkin' that's anything more than a TV show. Real life ain't like that."

"That's what Mom says, too."

Roger put his big hand on Carlos's head and gave it a good rub.

"Ouch. What did you do that for?"

"Just to let you know I love you."

Carlos rubbed his head. "Is this a guy thing? Mom would never do that."

"Yeah, guess she wouldn't. Sometimes guys have funny ways of showin' affection. It can embarrass us, you know. It's kinda how guys say I love you."

Carlos gave Roger a dirty look. "Come here."

Roger stooped down, and Carlos grabbed him around the neck. He rubbed his little knuckles over his father's head roughly. "Ouch," Roger said. "That hurt."

Carlos grinned. "And I love you, too."

Roger laughed and hugged his son. "I love you, son. I love you just because I can, and I do despite of faults, mistakes, or weaknesses."

Carlos rolled his eyes. "Dad, you were doing pretty good until you went there. I love you, too, the same way."

"Guess I had that comin'. Son, I want you to keep askin' questions, even the silly ones. It's the only way we learn. And I'll try to be patient with you. Deal?"

"Deal."

Roger could tell he had another question. "What is it?"

"Are you and mom gonna get together or what?"

Roger sighed. "Now that's a question we have to work on. You got to be patient. It's a complicated work in progress. I need to talk to her when she gets back. Okay?"

"Okay."

"I called the real estate agent about the property for sale. Mr. Rodriquez should be here soon to give me the details and show me where the boundaries are. If the price is right, I'm gonna buy it. I want to work around the house till he gets here. You can come along when he shows me, if you like."

"Think I'll pass, if that's okay."

"If you want. What are you gonna do instead?"

Carlos said. "Read."

"I should have known."

Mr. Rodriquez showed up promptly on time. Roger liked what he saw and heard about both properties for sale. A handshake, a check deposit, and a little paperwork finished their transition. A little recording at the County Court House, and it would be all his to do whatever, once he decided what whatever was.

***

"Ready or not, here we go, Carlos. Hope it goes well."

"Me, too."

They waited outside of Mrs. Porcher's house in Rockledge in Roger's truck.

"Bridget and Emily and Tricki Woo should be here soon. Cross your fingers, all goes well," Roger said.

Carlos crossed his fingers. A vehicle approached up Oakwood Drive from the street along the Indian River. and stopped next to them. They rolled their windows down. Roger said to Bridget, "Ready to do this just like we planned?"

She swallowed hard. "Yeah, let's do it. Tricki's getting anxious. He knows he's home."

"Good." They got out and walked to the house door with Roger and Bridget in front and the children behind them. Bridget carried a wiggly Tricki Woo in her arms. Roger knocked on the door hard.

Betty looked through the window and smiled. "Mrs. Porcher. They're here."

A moment later, Mrs. Porcher bounced out, beaming. "Oh! You're here. And with my Tricki Woo! I'm so happy." She took Tricki Woo from Bridget. He licked her face up and down.

"Tricki, you've been such a bad boy, running off like that, again, but momma forgives you. And you lost your collar, but never mind. I have what's really important, you." She turned to Bridget. "Oh, thank you so much. Roger told me how you found him at your farm." She glanced at the young girl behind her. "Is this Emily? Why, she's grown so much."

Emily gave a cute smile and waved.

Mrs. Porcher said, "Come Betty. Bring the subs I had James get from Publix and make sure you bring them all. I want everybody here to share in this glorious reunion, and I mean everyone. And some for Tricki Woo, too."

Betty smiled. "Yes, ma'am."

She got the sandwiches and James brought the drinks, gallon jugs of lemonade and sweetened tea, of course, along with plastic cups and paper plates.

All had a grand old time celebrating the return of Tricki Woo. Early the next day Mrs. Porcher sent James to the Melbourne

animal shelter to get the female Pekingese, the one Roger mentioned. She was still there unclaimed and running out of time. Another day and she would be put down. Tricki bonded with her quickly, and being Tricki, he tried to ride her, even if she was spayed.

Mrs. Porcher finally consented to having him fixed. He missed his family jewels for a while, and he never ran away again. He was quite happy with his new companion and, of course, Mrs. Porcher continued to pamper him lavishly his whole life which was long. He never wanted for anything ever. Going to the dogs worked fine for him, and Mrs. Porcher.

She soon loved the little female she named Shen Yeng as much as she did her Tricki Woo. Occasionally, he would wander for a day, but he was never lost. Tricki would always return. He knew where home was and where he was loved.

Chapter 39

It was late Friday afternoon when Gloria got to Roger's old trailer. The Police Academy Training Classes in Brunswick, Georgia, had let out after lunch. Nothing worse than releasing a bunch of hungry cops on the world. An accident on the bridge into Florida had traffic down to a crawl and progress was further delayed by construction on I 95 in Jacksonville. But she finally made it tired and a little cranky.

"How was the conference, Gloria?"

"Good. I learned a lot and made a lot of contacts. They showed us some of the newest gadgets, devices, and methods for crime investigation. It was well worth it."

"Glad to hear it. Carlos should be ready. We had some supper earlier. I wasn't exactly sure when your ETA was, so we made sure he was ready."

"Thanks. It's been a long day. Traffic was terrible. I'm not sure why it was this time of the year. Sometimes it just is."

"Yeah, traffics always terrible around Jacksonville. I expect it will get worse everywhere as the state continues to grow," Roger said.

"Mom! You're back," Carlos yelled. He rushed and hugged his mother.

"Oh, buddy. I missed you so. Did you have a good time with your dad?"

"Uh-huh. I had fun and learned a lot. Dad was a pet detective and found a lost dog."

Gloria smiled, "Interesting. That's a little out of your usual line. How did it go?"

Roger said, "You hit it on the head. Interesting. We, me and Carlos, got him back, and all ended well. And that's what's important."

"Anything else happen I should know?"

"Nothin' I care to go into now. How about soon?"

Gloria said, "Lunch on Sunday after church would be good. I could get some carry-in, and we could have it at my place. Carlos will be spending the afternoon with his friends he missed when I was gone. We need a long talk, and you know what it's about."

"I do. Consider it done. I'll see you Sunday."

Roger watched as the car carrying his son and Gloria disappeared down the road. He missed the kid already. Just having him there felt good. He liked the idea of being a dad.

"Grrrr."

"K9, what's up?"

"Grrrr."

A truck stopped in front of Roger's place. He rolled his eyes and mumbled, "Bill Kenney. I should have known."

Bill opened and closed the dummy-locked gate before driving up to Roger's trailer.

"Grrrr."

"I know you're feelin' better, K9, but bite him, and you'll feel bad again. You don't want to risk that."

Bill got out of his truck. "What's that you say, Roger?"

"I said I was just gettin' us some beers."

"Great idea."

When Roger came out of the trailer with two brewskis, he found Bill sitting in a chair with his hand raised waiting for the beverage.

Roger placed it in his hand.

Bill smiled. "You're welcome."

Roger groaned. "Did you come over to give me a hard time, or what?"

"It's a what. I got something for you, something you wanted, and asked for."

"What?"

Bill handed him a tissue wrapped small box.

"What is it, a box of Cracker Jack?"

"No, you galoot. Open it."

Roger parted the tissue paper and removed the lid of the gold-colored top. He parted an additional layer of tissue paper and found a badge. "Hey, this looks pretty nice."

"It was the most we could afford on our limited budget. And it probably won't turn your skin green, but I'll not guarantee it."

Roger looked it over carefully. It had a large six-pointed star in the middle with the name Canaveral Flats PD at the top. He rubbed his fingers over it and tasted them. "Nope, not a hint of caramel popcorn. This didn't come out of a Cracker Jack box."

"Roger, the mayor and I wanted you to look official and not rinky-dink if you're going to represent our town and area. We did have to try to economize a little. We paid by the letter. Note Police Department is abbreviated in bold letters only. And no periods after the letters. They were extra, too."

"That's still pretty nice. Hey, there's some more lettering under the star. It's small. Let's see, it says…SOB? Is this some kind of joke?"

"No, let me explain. We had to give you a title of some sort to make it official. We thought of two and chose this one. It's short for Special Operations Branch. It was between that and Special Homicide Investigation Team. We felt the first title better fit your position."

Roger thought for a moment out loud, "Special Homicide Investigation Team. Why, that would be S.H.I.T! I'm glad you didn't pick that."

"Yeah, we didn't like it either. And as I said, you do more than homicide, track down thieves, bank robbers, and even lost dogs. SOB, Special Operations Branch worked much better."

"Thanks a bundle. I guess I can live with it, considering the alternative."

Bill said, "We thought you'd feel that way. It's my understanding there's a group in a large city in the American Northwest saddled with the last title."

Roger laughed. "Better them than me. Thanks for small favors, buddy."

They made small chat as they sipped their beers. Roger asked again about the possibility of him really being at the top of the sheriff's list to head up the serial killer investigation, but Bill had heard no further information concerning it. It would work out one way or the other in time. Have patience.

After getting it all out, Bill left for home, leaving Roger to his thoughts. It had been an interesting week. First, the opportunity to help an old lady out by finding her missing dog, then Carlos showing up on his doorstep. That had worked out well. Better than he'd hoped. He liked the little guy and really enjoyed the company. Eva's showing up was a real surprise. He was glad she trusted him to be that open, but facing death together can bond people. And now he had a real badge. Just wait until the next yahoo gives him a hard time. He'll just show them.

Yeah, it would all work out, Lord willing, and the Creeks don't rise.

Chapter 40

Roger pulled into the parking lot of the Merritt Island garden apartment where Gloria lived. After finding a spot under a shade tree, he walked to her door and knocked. He heard noises behind the door. She opened it and said, "You're late."

"Yeah, traffic was heavy. Looks like there's some kind of rocket launch this afternoon. Can I come in or are you goin' to make me stand out here in the heat?"

"Sorry, come on in. I should have known. It did seem rather busy on the highway after church and when I picked up the carry-out. Hope you like Chinese? I picked up a Happy Family Dinner. It should have a little of something everyone would like."

Roger said, "Happy Family's good." He gazed around the apartment, neat, orderly, and clean, as he expected.

"Hungry?"

"Yuppers. I had a light breakfast. Wasn't hungry, but I am now. I could eat a horse."

She said, "No horse meat, and I hope no cat meat either."

"Huh?"

"A local Chinese restaurant was found to have cats in their freezer. You didn't hear about it?"

"No."

"It was a big brouhaha. They beat the rap by claiming it was for personal consumption and not to be sold at the restaurant."

"I missed it. I know I've been in countries where they often ate dog and cat, but I prefer my meal not to meow or bow wow at me."

She said, "I'm with you on that. Have a seat at the table. I'll heat the Happy Family up. It needs it after the wait."

Roger saw only two sets of plates and silverware. "Where's Carlos?"

"He's spending the afternoon with the friend he wasn't able to when I had to drop him off with you. I thought I told you."

"I would have liked to see him again."

Gloria said, "I thought as much, but you know how boys are. He wanted to spend time with his friend."

Roger said, "I think it's important I spend time with him."

"I know we can work something out. He had a good time while there, said you were a good guy and wanted to do it again. Please sit down. I'll heat this up and then we'll eat. Talk later."

Roger smiled and took a seat at the table. A minute later, he heard a ding, and Gloria came in carrying a dark carry-out container and a smaller paper box. She opened both, one containing the Happy Family and the other full of white rice.

Roger nodded, "Smells good."

218

"Like cat?"

"No, chicken, of course. It doesn't look like cat. Let's eat."

They filled their plates with what they wanted. The boxes were still about half full.

Roger said, "Looks like you have lunch for tomorrow."

"Thought I might. Didn't know how big an eater you were for sure, but I thought there'd be leftovers. Would you like some wine? I have a bottle of real peach-flavored wine. It's all-natural, nothing artificial."

"I think I'd like that."

She got up, returned with the wine, and poured some into their glasses. "There you go."

"Thank you." He took a sip. "This is good. I like it."

"I thought you would."

He laughed. "You're not plannin' on getting' me well lubricated and then havin' your way with me, are you?"

"Why, Roger, I'm shocked. To think you would think that of me."

"We do have a history, you know."

"Yes, I know. Every time I look at Carlos, I see you and remember."

"We need to talk about our plans for him."

Gloria said, "I know, but let's eat, Mr. Hungry Man. It's getting cold. It can wait till we've eaten."

Roger smiled and said no more.

The Happy Family was delightful, even after a little reheating. Roger added salt and pepper and a little duck sauce while Gloria put a generous amount of soy sauce on her food. They ate leisurely and made just a little small talk. Gloria filled their glasses again. Roger got a small second helping of the Happy Family. They finished and cleaned up the table. She put what was left in the refrigerator and topped off their glasses.

Gloria sat down in a chair to Roger's left. "Now, is there something you want to tell me?"

"We had an incident when Carlos was with me."

"Carlos got into your beer and got drunk."

Roger said, "How did you know?"

"He was acting guilty about something and spilled the beans. You know how it is. Little kids have a hard time keeping secrets, especially from their mother, and he had guilt written all over him. I knew something was up. I just had to get a confession as to what was up."

"I remember it well. At that age, I could never keep a secret from my mom, but I got better as time passed."

"Roger Pyles, I'm shocked. You? Keep secrets from your mother?"

"I'm glad she didn't find out all I did. I'd still be grounded, but don't you act so innocent. I know you were no saint, either."

She sighed. "Guilty as charged. Me and a couple of girl friends got into dad's liquor cabinet and got plastered, which wasn't difficult for a bunch of girls not used to alcohol. He read us the riot act and drove my friends home to their parents for their punishment. It's something I'll never forget. He made me tell them what we had done. I'm glad he was rough on us and made sure everyone arrived home safely. Some people aren't so lucky."

"I can tell there's more. What happened?"

"Guess you missed it, too."

"I've been playin' hermit for the last couple of days. No paper. No radio. Just nice and quiet."

She said, "Couple of underage teen girls from Titusville went to a party in Port St. John, got drunk, and attempted to drive home in the rain. They lost control of the car, spun out into a water-filled ditch, ended up upside down, and both drowned."

"How sad. How preventable."

She nodded. "Yeah. Are you in good enough shape to drive home? You don't have to. You can stay here."

Roger said, "If I didn't know better, I would think that has some undertones. Gloria, I know we have a history, but I don't want anything sexual to interfere and cloud our judgment on how we are to raise Carlos. That being said, I'm still in good enough shape to drive if I don't drink any more wine." He stopped and grinned. "And yes, you are a sexy woman, and I was a little temped, but I think it would be better if we don't pursue that line. We need to keep askin' ourselves what's best for him."

She was silent for a moment. "You're right. It's about Carlos, not us. How are we going to work this out?"

"I don't know. Let's continue on as we have been muddling our way through it until we come up with something better. It's worked so far."

"Guess you're right."

She grinned.

"Something funny?"

"Yeah, raising a child can have its moment." She stopped for effect. "Carlos has been learning about the animals on the African plain, prey and predator. You haven't lived until you've almost been knocked over by a young boy sneaking up on you from behind like a cheetah, flinging himself around your legs, growling, and saying, 'Die, gazelle, I got you.'"

Roger laughed. "That's funny. He never did that to me. Guess he must have thought I was more like a water buffalo and would throw him into a neighboring country. But we have had some fun."

"Yeah, like the poop like an Indian episode?'

Roger smiled. "That was a good one." He stopped. A serious look came to his face. "Now, I have a question for you. What inside information do you know about this high-level case I'm being considered for? Surely, you've heard something. Don't keep me in suspense."

"Sorry to disappoint you, but not much. I know about what you know. I've heard the scuttlebutt going around, but nothing concrete. You may want to talk to the Sheriff."

"I thought about that, but I'd rather wait until he approaches me. He could change his mind, or this could be all rumors."

"It's more than rumors, but the only one that knows the whole story is the Sheriff, and he's being very close-lipped."

Roger nodded. "Then I wait and go about my business."

"That's about it."

They sat in silence for a few moments. Roger sipped his wine and finished it. "Carlos is smart. He said his teacher called him a protégé, but I don't believe he understands all that involves."

Gloria said, "Yeah, he's very smart. I have trouble finding age-appropriate reading material for him. He's advanced in a lot of ways, but still just a kid and needs to do the things a young boy does, not be robbed of a childhood. And he's big for his age. Must take after you. His pediatrician says if he continues as the growth chart indicates, he should reach 6' 4", maybe even bigger."

"I'm about 6' 2". It wouldn't surprise me. Somehow, I guess we'll muddle along as best we can and hope for the best."

"In parenting and life."

Roger said, "Until we can see further down the road. One day at a time. Reminds me of something Pastor Nassey said, 'A light for my feet on the path in the darkness. Not a flood light piercing the night to see what lies far ahead.'"

"Guess so. So, where do we go from here?"

"Think I'm going home. If I stay here, we may both regret it in the long run. I'd better be goin'. Thanks for the lunch. Let's do it again and keep tryin' to resolve our Carlos dilemma we share."

Gloria said, "That we can agree on."

Roger got up and went to the door. "Guess I better go. Not sure how to part with the mother of my son."

"A hug would be nice, Roger."

Roger put his arms around her. It felt good. He could tell she enjoyed it. "I better go."

She nodded, but said nothing.

He walked to the truck and got in. Through the glass in her apartment door, Roger could see her watching him. A mischievous smile came to his face, and he winked at her.

She smiled and waved back. Roger could definitely get a girl's motor running.

He pulled out onto Courtenay Boulevard. Traffic was still heavy and crawling along. He used the time to consider the case coming up. Would he get it or not? What was it and was he up to a tough case yet? And what about Carlos? So many questions.

Traffic crept along. Southbound traffic seemed to have picked up, but northbound still crawled. As he went around a slight bend in the road, he saw the problem. Two alligators, one at least ten feet long and the other only slightly shorter, laid in the center turning lane like they owned it, and they hissed and snapped at any vehicle that got too close for comfort. Roger eased as far to the right as possible and passed by slowly on the shoulder. Only in Florida. First an elephant and now alligators. What next? A skunk ape, maybe. He didn't want to know. A nap was in order after the filling meal.

K9 was pretty well recovered, and he liked the air conditioning Lester installed. The property he'd bought had possibilities. Maybe, just maybe, he was becoming civilized. The rebel in him didn't like that idea. He had to do something wild and crazy. He smiled at the crazy thought that crossed his mind. Yes, that would do. Reality could wait. It would still be there tomorrow, waiting.

The ride to Canaveral Flats was uneventful. He stopped in front of his trailer to open the gate and noticed someone sitting in a chair on his porch. The hair on the back of his neck stiffened. His throat tightened. He relaxed when he realized the stranger was the

Shaman, the odd Seminole medicine man, who lived in the marshes along the St. John River. He'd been known to show up at the most curious of times.

Roger drove to the old trailer and got out. "Hello, Shaman. Make yourself at home, why don't you?"

The Shaman said nothing.

Roger opened the porch screen door, went in the trailer, got a beer, and sat down next to the Indian. "What brings you here? Seems when you show up, something's always about to happen."

"The Ancient Ones speak from pond. When you tell their story? They impatient. If you dead, their story not get told. They say you must be one tell it. Beware, Roger Pyles. Danger."

"Yeah, but that's behind me."

"No. Waiting. Be careful. Dead men tell no tales. Beware, Roger Pyles, if you want to live. Beware."

"Of what?"

The Shaman opened his mouth to speak, but closed it, got up, and left saying nothing leaving Roger startled. He'd no more than disappeared into swamp brush when a large black vehicle stopped in front of his trailer. A commanding voice came from its loud speaker, "Roger Pyles, stay where you are. We need to talk."

Roger yelled, "Who are you, and what do you want?"

WANT TO READ MORE?

Braddock's Gold Novels – Braddock's Gold, Hunter's Moon, Fool's Wisdom, and Killing Darkness

Florida Murder Mystery Novels – Death at Windover, Murder at the Canaveral Diner, Murder at the Indian River, Murder at Seminole Pond, Murder of Cowboy Gene, Murder in the Family, Murder the Most Dangerous Game, and Going to the Dogs.

Going to the Dogs is the eighth in the expanding *Florida Murder Mystery Novels*. Each book in the series is written as stand-alone novel. Readers say he keeps getting better. All of Mr. Heavner's twelve books can be found on Amazon as ebooks and paperbacks. The first book, *Braddock's Gold*, is also available as an audiobook from Audible at Amazon.

WANT TO HELP THE AUTHOR?

If you enjoyed the book, would you help get the word out? Please tell others about it. Word-of-mouth advertising is the best marketing tool on this planet.

A good review on Amazon, Goodreads, or elsewhere would also help the author be able to keep writing full time. It doesn't have to be long. Thanks.

SIGN UP FOR JAY HEAVNER'S NEWSLETTER

With this, Jay will occasionally keep you informed with new books coming out and anything else special. Feel free to email him at jay@jayheavner.com. His website is www.jayheavner.com. He loves reader feedback.

Made in United States
North Haven, CT
03 August 2022

22196437R00127